A Candlelight Ecstasy Romance®

"IF I WIN OUR RACE, I THINK I DESERVE A LITTLE MORE FROM YOU THAN JUST ANOTHER KISS," ROSS SAID, GIVING HER A SEXY GRIN.

"There's no point in worrying about it," Alix told him. "The only kiss you'll ever win from me is the one I've already given you."

"That just whets my appetite for you, Alix. And I'm sure you felt the same way."

"I did not. In fact, I've had much better," she lied as he came closer to her.

Suddenly his arm was around her and he pulled Alix to him, his mouth coming down on hers.

"We'll continue this at the finish line, captain," he said when their lips had parted.

CANDLELIGHT ECSTASY CLASSIC ROMANCES

THE TAWNY GOLD MAN, *Amii Lorin*
GENTLE PIRATE, *Jayne Castle*

CANDLELIGHT ECSTASY ROMANCES®

QUANTITY SALES

Most Dell Books are available at special quantity discounts when purchased in bulk by corporations, organizations, and special-interest groups. Custom imprinting or excerpting can also be done to fit special needs. For details write: Dell Publishing Co., Inc., 1 Dag Hammarskjold Plaza, New York, NY 10017, Attn.: Special Sales Dept., or phone: (212) 605-3319.

INDIVIDUAL SALES

Are there any Dell Books you want but cannot find in your local stores? If so, you can order them directly from us. You can get any Dell book in print. Simply include the book's title, author, and ISBN number, if you have it, along with a check or money order (no cash can be accepted) for the full retail price plus 75¢ per copy to cover shipping and handling. Mail to: Dell Readers Service, Dept. FM, P.O. Box 1000, Pine Brook, NJ 07058.

THE CAPTAIN'S WOMAN

Melanie Catley

A CANDLELIGHT ECSTASY ROMANCE®

Published by
Dell Publishing Co., Inc.
1 Dag Hammarskjold Plaza
New York, New York 10017

Dell ® TM 681510, Dell Publishing Co., Inc.

Candlelight Ecstasy Romance®, 1,203,540, is a registered trademark of Dell Publishing Co., Inc., New York, New York.

ISBN: 0-440-11007-8

Printed in the United States of America

September 1986

10 9 8 7 6 5 4 3 2 1

WFH

This book is dedicated to:

Hank Halsted,
for taking the time to demystify celestial navigation;
Alice Ashe,
for the friendship and love, and;
David Blanchard,
whose support and encouragement made all the
difference.

To Our Readers:

We have been delighted with your enthusiastic response to Candlelight Ecstasy Romances®, and we thank you for the interest you have shown in this exciting series.

In the upcoming months we will continue to present the distinctive sensuous love stories you have come to expect only from Ecstasy. We look forward to bringing you many more books from your favorite authors and also the very finest work from new authors of contemporary romantic fiction.

As always, we are striving to present the unique, absorbing love stories that you enjoy most—books that are more than ordinary romance. Your suggestions and comments are always welcome. Please write to us at the address below.

Sincerely,

The Editors
Candlelight Romances
1 Dag Hammarskjold Plaza
New York, New York 10017

THE CAPTAIN'S WOMAN

CHAPTER ONE

"We all *know* that women weren't meant to be captains."

Even in the dim light of the bar, the man's self-satisfied smirk was a beacon of gleaming white as he lounged back in his chair.

Not by the slightest twitch of her lips did the woman across from him betray her reaction.

Alexandra Boudreaux may have been visualizing Ross Morgan nicely breaded and fried to a golden crispy brown—*You turkey,* she thought with a silent, sardonic sniff—but no physical sign revealed it. Her slender fingers remained relaxed upon the cold slick curve of her glass. Only her eyes moved, zeroing in on the shadowed features across from her.

It was a strong, sure face, she reflected. A face that seemed carved from the elements. His skin was deeply tanned and lay over bones so sharp, so clean she couldn't shake the impression that nothing less than the scouring winds of a thousand ocean crossings could have honed them to such blade-thinness. If ever there had been softness in this man, none remained now. Even his hair was the hard pale silver forged of an unforgiving sun.

"This recent aberration"—he glanced around the crowded table, his blue eyes stopping on the equally sun-bleached head of his observer—"is no more lasting or meaningful than a Bahamian fog."

He paused.

In the silence the appreciative chuckle of the sailor beside him stood out clearly. As that sound died his eyes blatantly kept their focus on the face of the only woman at the table certified to command a ship.

With a grin that held more than a trace of the diabolical, he continued, "We have the proof of thousands of years behind us. Any language with the sense to identify nouns by gender uses the masculine for *captain*. A Frenchman would die before saying *ma capitaine*. Isn't that so, Ms. Boudreaux?"

Alix stared back.

He had been going on like this for the last fifteen minutes. Center stage, and loving every minute of it. While it was true that in order to be a good skipper one needed a strong sense of confidence, the ego of Captain Ross Morgan was off the wall. Somehow it was all the more infuriating to her that the monumental package of self-satisfaction before her came in such a devastating wrapper.

Thanks, Tully, she thought as she glanced at the man beside her. *You've really made my evening.*

From the moment her friend Tully had hailed the tall newcomer over to their table at Fort Lauderdale's well-known lounge Coconuts, and introduced her to the man with barely concealed anticipation as *Captain* Alexandra Boudreaux, this Morgan character had been riding a chauvinist bandwagon, singing out his foolish tune with verve and delight.

It galled her to the point that she was ready to show her contempt by getting up without another word and walking off. However, that particular satisfaction would preclude the even more heart-warming sight of Mr. Ego being humbled before his audience. So now she looked straight at his handsome face and curved her own well-shaped lips into a sweet smile.

"To tell you the truth, Captain Morgan, verbal game-playing with psuedointellectuals bores me stiff. Still, if you need an answer . . ."

Alix focused on her finger as it traced the rim of her glass. She waited another moment, apparently fascinated by the bubbles rising and bursting on the surface of her white rum and tonic. Then her eyes snapped up, catching his with a momentary blaze of green fire that she immediately banked.

"Allow me to suggest one word to you. *Hubris.*"

His white brows raised a millimeter, and Alix was sure she saw in his eyes a flash that could only be interpreted as pleasure.

So he knows the word, she thought. No surprise. He struck her as a walking, breathing example of hubris: overbearing pride. Indeed, someone arrogant enough to go up against the gods.

"A perfect choice, Alexandra. A woman attempting to take on a job that drives a man to the utmost of his limits strikes me as a classic example of presumption. And we all know pride goeth before a fall."

"You're implying that women can't help but fail the challenge?"

"Hell, it takes a special *man* to meet that challenge. What makes you think a woman, physically weaker and—"

"It takes," she interrupted with a firmness that allowed for no objections, "a special *person.* One who can handle the physical requirements of sailing a boat and dealing with the elements, who can meet the mental requirements of charting a course, and who possesses the strength of character needed to carry out the responsibilities of protecting the safety of the ship and the lives of everyone on board."

"I see." He sat back, one well-tanned hand going to his chin as he examined her.

"And I suppose you're one of those captains who feels the first requirement is filled by sitting back and ordering a burly crew to handle all the duties. Yeah"—he settled his elbow on the table, chin resting in hand as he stared across at her—"I guess it wouldn't take much muscle to play at captain, if that was your game."

"Charter passengers hardly qualify as burly crew," she answered back with a deliberate twist of amusement.

"And everyone at this table"—she looked around at the group of friends and acquaintances who seemed to be finding the conflict between her and Morgan fascinating enough to turn them all into a silent but appreciative audience—"knows how close to absolute zero the knowledge of some of these charterers is when it comes to sailing."

Her palm came down flat on the table and she leaned forward.

"Let me tell you, Morgan, when the man who's propped on the deck cushions beside you finds himself brought to the utmost of *his* limits by the challenge of keeping his martini balanced in a reaching sea, you'd damn well better be able to trim the sails yourself. And *I* can. I can change tacks while old Max is lifting his glass to his lips and he'll never lose a single drop of gin."

"You're talking a good game sitting here in Fort Lauderdale, safely berthed at Coconut's bar. But exaggeration is a sailor's stock in trade at the drinking table." Ross tipped his head to indicate a night-filled window and the ocean beyond. "When you're slipping over the Gulf Stream, that's when we see how much of your kind of talk translates into action."

He lifted his drink, saluting her with an insolent gesture.

"I suspect your little martini story would sink without a trace out there."

Again he moved his silver-blond head in the direction of the huge plate-glass window. The wall of moonless black there revealed only ghostly electric-blue glimpses of the night-shrouded Atlantic.

He was falling into it quite nicely, she thought. The hook had been set. Now she'd let her fish run with the line.

"The truth, Captain Ross, is the truth regardless of whether anyone accepts it."

"Well, let's have the entire truth then, Captain Alix. While you were busy winching in your genoa, there must have been a few moments when your eyes weren't glued to your martini-slugging passenger."

She grinned. Like a Cheshire cat she grinned. And the grin only became wider as an image came into her head of laboriously pumping her arm around and around as she reeled in rope holding a huge white sail. *Perfect.* It was time to haul in this barracuda and drop him flopping onto the deck.

"Yeah," she agreed. "If I was still back in the dark ages of sailing, I wouldn't have had the leisure to watch Martini Max. But the fact is, I had my eye on the guy start to finish."

With an exaggerated repeat of his earlier action, she lounged back in her chair and sent him a self-satisfied smirk.

"You see, Morgan, when you're sailing an unstayed rig, you don't have to bother with all that crap. My cat ketch has a self-tending jib. And let me tell you, it tends itself very smoothly indeed."

One corner of his mouth pulled up in a hard, contemptuous line.

"I should have guessed you'd buy into that lazy sailor's pipe dream."

His eyes raked her long-limbed form, assessing the legs in well-fitted white denim, the slender yet curved torso emphasized by a long-sleeved cotton jersey of watermelon red, the cocky tilt of her blond head. His irises were a hard-burning blue now as he seemed to catalogue her physical attributes. Those eyes seemed to be accusing her not only of having a body lacking the strength to handle a boat properly, but of having one much better suited to the bedroom.

"It's the kind of thing that would work on a woman—surface appeal. Looks over performance. It's going to kill you one day, lady."

With a harsh motion, he shoved his drink out of the way and leaned halfway across the table.

"You're going to be out on that ocean"—somehow his voice made it clear where she ought to be instead—"and the sea will show herself for the

17

jealous witch that she is. Then you and your toy boat will end up forty fathoms down."

Alix should have snapped back with a pithy rejoinder that showed his statement up for the exaggeration *it* was. But she found herself filled with such a mixture of confusion and indignation, she didn't know which emotion to respond to.

Unfortunately, confusion was winning out. The invisible current of sexual tension between them was sucking at her equilibrium like the undertow along a jetty, threatening to sweep her under. How could *she*—independent, intelligent Alix—be feeling sexual attraction for this close-minded egotist?

Unable to find a simple explanation, she grabbed for something to keep her afloat, and found her anger. Being angry was easy, much easier—and much quicker—than dealing with her complex, murky motivations. Opting for a "quick and dirty" response, she latched her indignation onto the first thing that came to mind.

"Toy boat!" For emphasis, she repeated herself. "Toy boat!"

"Toy. It's a Windsurfer, not a ship." Contempt laced each word. "To trust an unstayed rig beyond protected waters is insane."

On the verge of another outburst, Alix stopped. Anger was one thing. Uncontrolled anger was another. Alix reined herself in a bit and focused on her goal here—winning the argument.

"My," she returned with a coolness she was nowhere near feeling, "so that sounds defensive, Captain. Maybe too defensive?"

She was leaning forward herself now, both arms on the table. All the others at the table were stretching their necks, intent upon the conflict. Beside her, Tully had a sparkle in his eye that had last been seen when he was watching the fifth round of the world heavyweight championship.

Her lips curved into a smooth, condescending smile. "Sounds like you're afraid of anything new," she said.

"Afraid? The word is *smart,* woman. Smart. I'm not going to throw *my* life away on some idiotic aberration."

"There's that word again. Anything that doesn't fit in your narrow little world you call an aberration."

"Think about it. Your boat absolutely has to be strong—and I mean *massively* strong—at the partners. If the spot where the mast meets the deck isn't the strongest part of your boat, you won't *have* a boat. The stress of that swaying spar will rip it apart. Is that any way to build a boat?"

She was about to answer, but he never gave her the chance. The man had firmly planted himself on his soapbox, and he was on a roll.

"Over two thousand years of performance proves stayed rigs work. As long as your wires are in good shape, you ain't never gonna lose that mast. Maintain the stays—you do agree that maintaining the equipment of your vessel is only good seamanship?—and it can't break, it can't fall."

Ross's arm waved in an end-of-argument gesture. But he didn't stop talking. "And speaking of seamanship, it isn't seamanlike to have your mast waving around at the whim of the wind."

"Tell me," she slipped in as he paused to draw breath, "do you wear suspenders and a belt?"

"Of course not. That's a stupid analogy. It doesn't—"

"No it isn't."

Alix spoke with the same iron voice that sent reluctant male crew members scurrying to obey an order. She'd conceded the floor to this man long enough. It was time for the clock to start on her rebuttal, and she had a few points to make clear.

"Suspenders and a belt used to be necessary to keep up a pair of trousers—then tailors learned to design trousers better. Unstayed masts are a better design. The world does march on, Ross Morgan, whether you like it or not."

She moved her right hand as though sweeping the decks clear.

"Clumsy, awkward design must give way when something better comes along. Do you know how much space I gain below decks? Without the heavily reinforced chain plates"—she referred to the equipment that held in place the wires that steadied the mast—"there's a lot more room to

20

stow things. Even the layout can be more comfortable and spacious."

Now Alix needed to draw breath. As she did they stared at one another.

Somehow the look that passed between the two acknowledged that the fight wasn't really over ship design. There was a deeper, more elemental conflict between them. Their opposing positions on unstayed masts was certainly nothing more than a symbol of the differences between them.

Not the least of the problems was the fiery man-woman response that angered even as it lured. Alix knew lovemaking was sometimes depicted as a battle between the two sexes, and she could well imagine the intensity with which this man would wage it. In fact, unbidden images of just how that battle might be executed suddenly flooded her mind, nearly taking her breath away.

No. She denied the images. *NO.*

Don't let yourself surrender this way. Don't let mere physical attraction cloud your mind and weaken you. You must be strong, she ordered herself, every bit as strong as he is. Stronger.

A woman had to be strong. She had to take care of herself, and then she had to dig down deeper to find within herself the strength to look out for others as well.

That was the way of the world, Alix knew. It's what her mother had had to do when she was left alone to raise two children. It was what Alix herself had had to do when her mother finally collapsed of overwork, and the support of the family fell to her.

She stared at Ross Morgan. Women were weak? She knew the truth from hard, bitter experience. Women endured.

"Well, I always thought," broke in Tully, "that I should sail a stayed rig downwind. But an unstayed rig upwind. Think I could talk a race committee into that combo?"

At the unexpected intrusion into the silence, Alix severed eye contact with Ross to look at her friend. It was obvious he was trying to rescue the table from the awkward pall that had fallen over it while she and Ross stared at one another. It was also obvious—to her, at any rate—that Tully was being prodded by a little guilt at having deliberately initiated the clash.

Go ahead and feel a little guilty, she thought with affectionate amusement. *After all, you did want to see the sparks fly, Tully. So what you're feeling now is nothing more than the just pay that you owe in return for your little bit of entertainment.*

"I'll tell you what, Tully. I want to be a fly on the wall when you try and put *that* argument to Commodore Billings," hooted one of the other men.

"I've never sailed with an unstayed mast," a small brunette remarked, joining in. She looked to her companion. "You sailed a Freedom yacht once, didn't you, Joe? What do you think?"

As the rest of the group took up the issue, the conversation flowed on around Alix and Ross. She was content to let it. So, apparently, was he.

I wonder what he's thinking?

She couldn't read the man. That connection between them a moment ago was gone. His thoughts were his own again, shut behind the wall of his will. Instead, his gaze was probing hers. Would those intense blue eyes of his pierce her carefully shielded thoughts?

". . . easily managed sail area. Of course there's the self-tacking, as Alix pointed out. So it's very easy sailing. I liked the hassle-free . . ."

I wonder what she's thinking?

Ross continued to watch Alix. But her eyes were like polished jade—smooth and cool and opaque. Nothing came through. And he knew it was because she intended nothing to.

Beneath the table his hand tightened into a fist over one thigh of his camel-colored sailing shorts. What are you really like, Captain Alexandra Boudreaux? Hard. Or soft? Fire. Or ice? Powerful. Or weak?

One thing he knew that she was, was intelligent. Though she hadn't realized he was putting her on with his macho male remarks about women captains, it was no reflection on the woman's quickness of mind. No one ever caught him playing his put-on game until he allowed them to. The act was perfect. Of course it could be a dangerous sport. But then, nothing in life that had any flavor to it was easy.

Making love to this woman wouldn't be easy.

There would be an exhilaration that would more than compensate, though, of that he was certain. Wild, powerful—the experience would have to be as intense as facing a storm on the open seas alone.

He had sought out the challenge of setting himself against the might of the sea. Was this challenge one that he wanted to pursue?

Was the game worth the candle? he thought as the conversation continued around him. Or would he find himself caught in messy emotional entanglements that would outweigh the pleasure of bringing this woman to his bed?

Again Ross's eyes traveled over Alix, who had turned her attention to the lively discussion volleying around her.

There was an alert look on her tanned face. A face, he noted, of surprisingly elegant planes. It was intriguing how their aristocratic lines juxtaposed with the short hair that curled over her head. The tumbling loops had the same wild grace that was seen on statues of ancient Greek youths.

Now she looked relaxed, natural, yet she radiated a leashed energy that reminded him of a snow leopard at rest. Her right hand lay in a casual curve around her empty glass, and like the faint flip of a leopard's tail, one thumb was absently caressing its water-beaded surface.

The habit was a common enough one. But where that action would come across in most people as a fidgeting, meaningless gesture, Ross could see that in Alix the slow, steady sweep of the tanned finger reflected an unconscious sensuality, a sureness and sense of self so deep it was inherent in her every motion.

He found himself mesmerized by that rhythmic movement. His attention locked onto her thumb.

In that instant—in the space of time it took to make one downward sweep—Ross knew.

By the time she was on the slide upward, he was already committed to the challenge.

And as she once more started the slow motion downward, he was prepared to face whatever consequences came his way in order to win Alexandra Boudreaux into his bed.

CHAPTER TWO

Ross contemplated the woman he was planning to love with a thoroughness that should leave them both breathless.

She didn't look particularly receptive.

Those cool, cool green eyes had caught him staring once more. One glance into them and it was obvious that despite the sexual attraction that had arced between them earlier, her intellect was in full command here, and *it* was saying, "Not interested."

Actually, that was good.

Yes, he repeated to himself, it was good. It meant there was less chance of running into that emotional entanglement he was concerned about.

Now, if he was looking for an affair of any length of time, it would be different. The odds wouldn't be nearly so good, even given her antipathy for him. Continued physical closeness could so easily lead to emotional closeness, and, conversely, emotional dislike could lead to physical rejection. But liking wasn't a requisite to "loving" in the physical sense. Hadn't he known a number of people who couldn't stand each other outside of bed, but who managed to find a special harmony between the sheets?

Of course he had. And as he'd already determined, just a night or two with Alix would do. Actually, one night was all he needed to answer those questions that would be haunting him until they were resolved.

And, Ross reminded himself as he leaned back into his chair and lifted his glass, the sooner he started exploring those questions, the sooner he would be getting his answers.

Question number one was how to reestablish— he mentally chuckled—a meaningful dialogue with the woman. Taking a healthy swig of his drink, he set the glass down on the table.

"So how the hell do you reef a wishbone jib, anyway?"

Her eyes widened, and he felt a small rush of satisfaction. His shoulders moved lazily as he elaborated on the challenge he'd thrown her.

"Say a line squall blows up. There you are, smack in an unsafe situation." Large tanned hands lifted as though presenting her with his conclusion. "QED unseaworthy."

He watched her find her footing on the tilting deck of their discourse. Somehow he sensed that that mental agility of hers would be more than matched by a physical one.

"Well, I'll tell you, old salt," she was saying to him, "when the wind leaps up from fifteen knots to twenty-five"—she folded her arms and settled in her seat—"I simply lean back and savor the sight of my ship taking care of herself. And what do I see? My carbon-fiber mast bending."

She drew a breath and smiled sweetly. "Now—and I hope this bit of physics doesn't tax you beyond your capacity to understand—that flattens the sail, which in turn spills air from it.

"So there I am"—her smile turned puckish—"cruising along, all nice and slowed down without lifting a finger. No need to go madly scrambling around trying to tie down whipping canvas in order to reduce my sail area."

A laugh broke from her as she tossed his own salty language back at him. "Hell, turkey, I don't have to think of reefing until after you're tucking in your *second* reef."

"A-ha." He pounced on her statement. "You've just admitted there that you do have to reef. And you never answered my question about how you do it."

"When the winds *finally* become heavy enough that even my setup requires reefing," she replied, unfolding her arms, "I don't do it a bit differently than you, Ross."

Her hand made a little unwrapping gesture. "I just slack the halyard"—she referred to loosening the wire that held the top of the sail to the top of the mast—"pull and fold the sail, and tie down the folds."

"Fine. But that still leaves you needing a storm

trysail," he objected. "With full reefing, it's not necessary. The third reef is enough to get the sail area down to a size that lets it serve as a storm sail."

"Aarggh." Alix looked heavenward. "You're hopeless."

"No. I'm a purist."

As he grinned she muttered under her breath, "And a sexist."

His grin became more diabolical. "Try me."

"You wish."

The tone of her voice left little doubt as to her opinion of his offer. Lord, the man was infuriating. *I'll bet he thinks he's a fabulous lover too.*

"What's the matter? All talk and no action?"

She sent him her lethal-at-fifty-paces stare. "What do you mean?"

"You keep telling me what a great sailor you are. Let's see some money on the table."

"Okay." Her words slid out on a weary, resigned sigh. "What are you driving at?"

"You and me." His statement dropped into newly minted silence as the rest of the table tuned into round two of the Morgan-Boudreaux bout. "I know I'm the better sailor. But if you *think* you are, then prove it."

"You want a race?"

He nodded. "No crew. Just you and your boat, me and mine."

"When?"

"You name it, lady. I'll be available."

"At loose ends, are we, Captain?" The tip of her index finger made a complete circuit of the rim of her glass. "Your services not being snapped up?"

He loosed a sardonic snort. "Ross Morgan is always in demand. I pick and choose."

"And right now you 'choose' not to work?"

"Right now I'm gearing up for a season of chartering in the Caribbean. But *I'll* decide when I go. So how about it? Ready to back up your high-flying talk and accept the challenge? Or is it too much for you?"

Though Alix felt her temper rising into the red zone, she controlled it. Impulse urged her to snatch up the gauntlet he'd thrown at her, but she knew she needed to consider more than her own satisfaction. She stalled for time.

"Where are you berthed?"

"South of Las Olas Bridge. And you?"

"Las Olas?" she said derisively. "The low-rents hang out there. Shoot, that's just one step above the Singapore Fleet."

Her reference to the shabby houseboats that filled Singapore's harbor did not go unnoted. "And where are you?" he asked with equal sarcasm. "In the River Bend Yacht Basin?"

She shrugged her shoulders, acknowledging she was berthed in the up-scale mooring.

"I should have known." He lapsed into disgusted silence.

Alix took advantage of the quiet to consider his

challenge. She was burning with the desire to show up this cocksure captain. But to do so would mean abandoning her responsibilities. Today was Tuesday. She was slated to set sail for the Caribbean Thursday, and she had more than a full day's worth of preparations to complete. It boiled down to responsibility versus personal desire, and she knew which had to lose out. She didn't have to like it, though.

"Much as I would dearly love to beat you—and I *would* beat you—I can't take the time to race. I have obligations, my schedule is too full."

"Sure."

Her brow raised. "As I've said before, the truth is the truth whether anyone believes it or not. I have to provision. I'm setting sail for St. Thomas on Thursday."

"St. Thomas?"

A speculative look crossed his face. "You going to be there long?"

"Yes and no."

She watched him fold his arms and wait for her to explain. She was tempted to just let the statement hang, but then she decided that was a childish action. "I'm sailing there. Then I'm booked to handle a few charters myself in the Antilles. But I'll be back for the Charter Boat League Annual Regatta."

"Will you? Planning on amazing us all by winning that one?"

"As a matter of fact, I will."

31

Silently Alix repeated, *You bet I will. And when I do, it will prove to everyone that women are as skilled at the art of sailing as any man. That will be the real prize; the money's just frosting on the cake.*

She'd been waiting a long time to enter that regatta as a charter captain and prove her worth. Winning it over this arrogant man sitting across from her was going to make a sweet victory all the sweeter.

He was looking around the table. "The lady is so confident, everybody. Well, I hate to burst your bubble, Alix, but I'll be in that regatta too."

"Fine." She also looked around the table, making sure her audience was listening. "You want to race? Let's just see which one of us walks off with the league trophy and the prize money."

"Uh-*uh.*" He shook his head emphatically. "I want our competition to be one on one."

He lapsed into silence and his gaze lost its focus. After a moment a smile spread across his face. It made his earlier diabolical grin look like the gentle beaming of a baby in his mother's lap.

"Ms. Captain Boudreaux, I think I have the perfect solution. And the perfect stakes."

"Do you now?"

She tossed him a skeptical glance. If this man thought it was perfect, then his "solution" was almost guaranteed to be spelled t-r-o-u-b-l-e.

The light caught again in his silvery hair as he

leaned forward. "I propose a single-handed race—"

"Surprise," she interrupted dryly.

He forged on. "The stakes to be as follows—the loser will crew for the winner when *he* races in the Charter Boat League Annual Regatta."

There was a murmur of appreciation around the table, in which Alix was tempted to join. How fitting for the winner to have the loser at *her* beck and call, for the losing skipper to be forced to help his rival win the regatta, she thought.

"And this race?" she drawled.

"The ideal test," he replied. "A half-day's sail is no measure of the ability of a sailor. It takes a voyage for that—a long voyage."

Ross tilted back in his chair. He stayed that way, his stance cocksure and arrogant. Then suddenly the chair banged down on the floor. In a smooth sweep he let the forward momentum send him across the table, his forearms planted flat, his shoulders hunched forward. The searchlight-blue eyes impaled her once more.

"We're both headed in the same direction. I challenge you to race me from here to the Virgin Islands."

CHAPTER THREE

It was crazy. Absolutely crazy.

It was insane to race a boat hundreds of miles —alone—for the sake of ego.

"You got it."

Alix reached across the table and took Ross's hand in a firm shake. She nodded her head for emphasis. "I'll meet you at the start Thursday morning. Agreed?"

"Agreed." He lifted his chin to look over at Tully, who was totally absorbed in the exchange. "And this man is hereby appointed head of the race committee."

"Excellent choice," approved Alix.

"Hey, wait a minute, guys." Tully got a distinctly cornered expression on his face. "I don't think—"

"Oh, *I* do, Tully. Don't you, Ross?"

"Without question," he concurred. They both grinned at the man who had instigated the evening's conflict.

"Why, it's only fitting that our friend Tully here, who was so anxious to get us together"—

Alix threw Ross a look that was received, approved, and returned: *We* know *what this man's motive was*—"should share in the outcome of that meeting."

Another look passed between her and Ross. This one triggered a grin as she remembered an old Arabic saying: "I against my brother; my brother and I against my cousin; my cousin and I against the world."

That maxim fit this situation like a glove. She and Ross were enemies—she couldn't ever imagine getting along with the man—but an outside force had "conspired" against them, and they would join forces for an appropriate payback. Her grin still in place, she turned to the round, apprehensive face of the man who barely a half hour ago had been taking such delight in tossing her into the lion's den.

"Yes, my friend, you'll be responsible for arranging this race—and of course you'll serve as the 'umpire' for all protests."

"Decide who's right," elaborated the captain, managing to appear very large and very strong as he sat opposite Tully, "and who's wrong."

With the subtle emphasis he'd placed on the last word still ringing in Alix's ears, he deliberately captured Tully's gaze and directed it toward Alix.

"Enforcing the decisions, upholding the one in the right," Alix added, boring into her friend's eyes with an intense look.

"Well, of course, normally I'd be honored," he replied in a voice that left some doubt as to his total enthusiasm for the role, "but—"

"No, Tully." Ross's impressive shoulder line loomed across the table. "This is important to us."

Alix followed suit, leaning on Tully's arm. "You wouldn't disappoint me. Not when *you* are the reason this race has come about."

Tully blanched.

Ross looked blandly at Alix. "I think our friend is overwhelmed."

"He's carrying a heavy responsibility."

Alix's solemn mien was just a shade too good to be true, and the fact that the corners of her lips kept threatening to quirk into a grin didn't help the sincerity quotient much either.

"And so little time for him to organize things," sympathized the captain.

"You're so right, Ross."

Alix beamed at him. Standing up, she slipped her hands under Tully's arm and tugged. "Tully's going to have to begin right this minute to get it all done in time."

"But I just started this drink," protested the suddenly unmovable object.

"Priorities, Tully, priorities."

The man's pudgy one hundred and eighty pounds of resistance hugged his chair. He intended to stay put.

But leverage has always been able to turn unmovable objects into movable ones. When Ross joined Alix and set his hands underneath Tully's other arm, they found themselves able to lift him —chair and all.

"Drop it," Ross ordered.

And Tully, after a few seconds of stubborn inaction, loosed his fingers from their grip on the seat. The chair clattered to the floor.

Smoothly whisking him away from the fallen seat, his feet not even touching the floor, she and Ross exchanged a grin over the balding top of Tully's head.

"Say good night to the folks, Tully," she ordered sweetly.

Red was creeping up his neck and had just reached his cheeks when the man suddenly burst out with a laugh.

"Well, I guess it's worth it," he said. "I guess a few minutes of humiliation is little enough to pay for the pleasure of watching you two egomaniacs slug it out. But I expect danger pay if I have to stand between you."

Once more wordless communication passed between her and the silver-haired captain.

Three seconds later Tully discovered himself on the finishing end of a bum's rush as he was set down beside his car outside Coconut's.

He took one look at the expressions on the faces of his two "bouncers" and all his bravado melted like ice cream on a Miami sidewalk in June. He practically leapt into his car.

"Tomorrow afternoon, Tully, I expect a full report on the race setup," warned Ross, the white tufts of his eyebrows working in a menacing fashion.

"Ditto, my friend." Hands on her hips, Alix clearly meant business.

Nervously nodding his head, the man fumbled his key into the ignition. Another moment and all Alix could see of him was the red glow of his taillights as he flew out of the parking lot.

Simultaneously she and Ross burst into laughter.

"Do you believe the way he held on to that chair?" he gasped.

She was laughing so hard her stomach hurt. "I'll bet he sets a new land record getting home tonight."

"Barnacles have less sticking power than that man's hands," Ross declared between helpless hoots.

"And the look on his face . . . when you said . . . you said . . . decide who's . . . right . . . and who's wrong . . ."

Alix was totally out of breath, weak with laughter. She and Ross were staggering about in the dark parking lot, barely able to stand up. Blindly she put out a hand to steady herself.

At first she connected with nothing but air. Then her unseeing action put her in direct contact with the firm wall of Ross's chest.

For a moment she didn't realize what had happened. It felt so natural, that physical contact, like this was a body she had known for years. She was so caught up by the ease of the moment and the feeling of familiarity that without thinking she leaned into Ross for support.

His arms curved—as automatically?—around to support both their laughter-weakened bodies. Awkwardly they clung to one another, a mutual gesture of aid and camaraderie.

The easiness of it all, the rightness deepened into a warm glow for Alix. And from that warmth it began to stir just as naturally into the first siren calls of desire.

That was an emotional/mental sensation, but there was a matching physical sense. His body was warm, yet not too warm, on this South Florida night in early November. Beneath the cotton jersey shirt he wore his flesh was firm as only that of one who uses his body to make his living can be. One hard, strongly muscled thigh pressed against her. Yet, strangely enough, what was most erotic was the feel of his fingers as they bit into her upper arms in an attempt to support her weight.

Alix was giddy from lack of breath. She was still helplessly gasping out the last of her amusement. But she was, as ever, captain of her ship—even when that ship was her own body.

She was feeling some unexpected emotions, and certainly some confusion, but she did not feel out of control.

At the moment she was faced with two options in this situation. She could break things off now, and restore the relationship to its true balance— that of adversaries. Or she could allow herself to explore for a few minutes longer these oh-so-pleasant sensations. If she did choose that path, she knew she could do so without sacrificing the even balance of power currently existing between them.

As Ross's grip changed subtly, she knew that he was already making his decision on the issue. She did want to satisfy this sensual curiosity. She could follow his lead . . . or she could chart the course herself.

And that is precisely what Alix proceeded to do.

Swinging her head up, she captured his unprepared lips with a sudden kiss. There was no hesitation, no holding back. She wanted to know, and she was going straight for the answer.

Ross's response was equally that of one used to command.

A flicker of time was spent in registering the unforeseen event. Another instant or two followed, which—from the sense of distraction she noted—must have been used in examining his alternatives. Then Alix found her domination of the kiss challenged.

He went after control with a skill that would have left her breathless with admiration if she'd allowed herself time to absorb it. But Alix was not one to ease back from a challenge.

Dueling lips, she thought with amusement as she plunged into the contest.

Her fingers curled up into the silver thatch and found it surprisingly soft. The strands slid over her fingers like cool silk, adding another sensual thrill to the ones being evoked by his smooth lips. She pressed closely, discovering that their tall, lean bodies fit together remarkably well. As he tightened his embrace, that fit only came closer and closer to perfection.

Before the traitorous sound touched off by those sensations could escape, Alix caught the tiny moan welling up in her throat. In compensation, her kiss grew more intense—as did Ross's.

She found herself literally growing faint from the stimulation and sensed that Ross was reacting the same way.

It was too much. She needed to draw away, to allow the tumultuous sensation to settle. Yet she couldn't be first. Wasn't that tantamount to conceding victory to him on this score?

Her entire body was buzzing with an effervescent wine of desire that grew ever stronger. She couldn't, she couldn't keep it up. She had to stop.

But how in the world was she going to get out of this the winner that she had to be?

Her lips were already slipping away from Ross's, the defeat filling her with its bitter taste, when Alix realized that she had this completely wrong.

It wasn't defeat at all.

No, to break away from this mesmerizing kiss first was to show not weakness but strength. To show that she was less affected by the caress than was he.

The pleasure this thought brought to her reached her lips in the form of a smile. But the smile froze as it crossed her mind that she needed to make the fact clear to Ross. After all, he could have the mistaken idea that her stopping first was a display of weakness. Which she now knew was absolutely untrue.

She continued to hold tightly to that thought, ruthlessly squelching the faint voice at the back of her mind that said Ross's kiss had undone her.

How was she to get her message across to Ross? she wondered as she stepped out of his arms. Deftly she turned away from his probing eyes. The soft ocean breeze cooled her face.

In an instant, she had it.

"Well. Fun, Captain." She laughed, looking back, the laughter floating over her shoulder.

"We'll have to try that again sometime." She couldn't resist a sexy little flip of her hips as she started off. "Perhaps when you congratulate me for winning the race."

And she sauntered toward Coconut's entrance.

Ross was beside her in a second. His eyes were dark, glittering, their color lost in the harsh glare of the parking-lot lights. What wasn't lost was the strength of feeling there. But whether his emotion was desire, or anger, or both, or even a multitude of other ones, she couldn't tell.

"Just a kiss?"

His voice sounded cool and amused, belying the burning brightness of his eyes.

As he walked he could sense his body echoing with the feel of Alix—the press of her thighs against his, the yielding warmth of her back filling his arms, the softness of her breasts tight against his chest. The touch of her lips was still throbbing on his mouth. And the hands swinging at his side remained loosely cupped, as though those fingers still held her tantalizing curves.

He had to fight the impulse to yank her back into his arms. More than anything in the world at that moment he wanted to explore all the wonders of her body. But he couldn't betray his weakness. He had to keep control. With a woman like her, he couldn't show any trace of vulnerability. It would be fatal. But that didn't mean he couldn't show his sexual interest. He didn't have to hide that he wanted her, only that it mattered to him.

"Don't you think the victor might feel that after winning such a long race, he deserved a *little* more than a kiss?"

His lips quirked in a sexy grin. He walked with an easy rolling motion, the movement of a man who was in command of his body.

Alix had to look away from the motion. It was too uncomfortably alluring, and it brought to mind physical prowess in more intimate endeavors than sailing. His taunting question brought vividly to mind an image of the two of them making love. She was shocked by how that image electrified her with a deep, piercing sense of need.

Her body was mutinying against reason, and it angered her. If libido alone were ruling her, she would be agreeing right then and there to raise the stakes on their wager to include a night of lovemaking. But Alix was always aware that actions carried consequences. Responsible adults had an obligation to examine those consequences before acting.

The consequences of that were too high a price. If she won, it would be all right—making love to this man would be her option. She would be in control. But if she lost, then making love with him would be surrender. And Alix Boudreaux never surrendered. She always won.

Tonight she was going to win too. She knew— if she would face the fact, and she had to—that she wanted Ross Morgan. Fine. She would accept that. But the scales had to balance. He had to want her too.

"One kiss isn't enough, huh?" she challenged with a sexy laugh. Her head tipped back to direct his sight to where they'd been standing. "That kiss wasn't enough?"

"Did you think so?" he countered.

"I've had better," she lied.

"You started it, Captain. I think the responsibility for the quality lies with you."

"Maybe you're just slow getting started," she mused aloud, as if he had never said a word. "I wonder if that's true in your sailing as well?"

"Cheap talk again."

His lips tightened in annoyance, and his back seemed to stiffen slightly. She watched his hair turn from glowing silver to misty gray as his steps moved him beyond the range of the parking-lot light.

"Talk, with no action to back it up," he said after a few seconds.

He strode another two feet, then stopped dead in his tracks, his hands shoved in the pockets of his sailing shorts. He swung around. "Care for a rematch?"

She laughed as she drifted to a halt in front of him.

"Willing to lose again, are you?"

"I think we know who'd lose."

Her reply came from deep in her throat. "Do we?"

The wicked little chuckle with which she followed her question died an early death as Ross seized the initiative.

His arm was hard like iron around her as he pulled her to him, his mouth a driving, searing force upon her lips.

Deliberately Alix allowed herself to soften in

45

his arms, to seem to surrender to his power. That move would grant her the element of surprise when she took control in a few moments, she told herself. As his mouth continued its sensual assault she softened further, her body molding itself to his.

She returned his passionate caresses as she clung to him, her hands cupping and kneading the broad shoulders, drinking in the strength through her fingertips. She felt as if they were welded together, the heat of their bodies sending her blood racing.

His arms were moving now as he kissed her, his hands sweeping down her back in masterful strokes. As their tongues joined in wild dueling, all warm velvet and satin, Alix experienced waves of desire radiating from deep within her, driving her onward. His tongue brushed against the sensitive roof of her mouth; she arched in response, then began an exploration of her own that drew a soft moan from deep in his throat.

An already crushing embrace tightened even more, and her hips moved against him in an unconscious, gently urging motion as they held one another with all the strength that passion could empower.

In her mind there was no plan anymore, no objective, no world—only desire and sensation.

It was only when they broke apart that Alix remembered she had been intending to seduce him. To drive him crazy. Yet she was the one who had ended up mindless with desire.

She stared at Ross. There in his face she saw the truth. Yes, she had been swept away by desire, but no more than had he.

She had achieved her objective. She had wakened a demon in this arrogant, dynamic man of the sea.

The knowledge was small comfort as Alix realized that in kindling the fire in Ross Morgan, she had caught herself in the same all-consuming flames.

CHAPTER FOUR

"Fair wind, fair sailing."

The words floated softly on the breeze as Alix released the full breath she'd drawn. Her body tingled with a pleasure composed of one part clean, crisp air, one part sunshine and sea, and three parts anticipation. Arms lifted high, she hauled down on the halyard line. It was a good feeling, a familiar feeling.

"Stand by on that sheet," she called out.

His pudgy hand just a patch of flashing white in the brilliant early morning sunlight, Tully waved back acknowledgment of her order. His other hand gripped the thick rope to which she was referring.

Eyes greener than the water scanned the flat horizon to the east, studying the sky. Yes, it's a good day for starting a passage, she thought with satisfaction.

Ten busy minutes later, Tully asked, "Are you sure you want to do this?"

She looked at him with mock exasperation.

"Because we can always just chalk this whole

crazy idea up to a few too many drinks the other night, you know."

"I wasn't drunk. And neither was Ross." She put a hand on his shoulder and grinned. "I can't speak for you."

"Had to be," he admitted. "Or nothing could have gotten me to say I'd referee this prizefight."

With a short, silvery laugh, Alix dropped her hand. Prizefight. Tully didn't know how apt his metaphor was. She recalled the "prize" that had been on her mind, and Ross's, the other night. With a tense little motion, she shook *that* thought out of her head.

"Time for me to cast off, Tully."

"Honestly, Alix. Single-handing is no picnic at any time. And pushing yourself with a race when you don't need to—"

"Who says I don't need to?"

"Oh, great." He threw up his arms and turned within the confines of the small cockpit, his deck shoes squeaking a protest. "The old competitive spirit claims another victim."

"So? I like challenges. You like practical jokes. To each his own, Tully."

"Well," he said as if speaking to himself, "I wouldn't try to shift the Rock of Gibraltar. So how could I have been foolish enough to offer advice to Alexandra Boudreaux?"

"To know one's own mind is a strength, Tully."

"Lots of things are strengths until they're carried too far."

"Even advice-giving. Now scoot."

Cheerfully she took him by the arm and led him to the gunwales. "Get off my boat. You have to get your committee boat out to the start."

"Some committee boat. An old Cigarette with an oversupply of party-happy sailors."

"What are you complaining about? Partying is your strong suit."

She watched him push off from the railing and land not so lightly on the dock.

"Now," she said as he turned to face her, "you remember the times that we've set up for the radiophone, don't you?"

"You check in with me at nine and twenty-one hundred hours," he answered as he loosened her mooring line, "and Ross calls at ten and twenty-two hundred." He coiled the thick rope in his hands, keeping tension on it until it was time to toss it onboard.

"Well." Alix stepped to the wheel. "This is it, Tully." As she steered, the boat slowly began to slip away from the dock. "Wish me luck."

"Luck?" he called as he arced the looped line through the air. It landed with a heavy thud on the teak deck. "Alix, honey, I hope you beat the pants off him."

Laughing, Alix swooped past Ross's boat, her white sails flashing in the sun.

"Not bad," she teased, "for an antique!"

The wind carried her words across to him. The grin she received from him in return, along with a hand casually flipped in greeting as the two boats whizzed past each other, was one of sardonic good humor.

The man had the same sparkle in his eyes that Alix knew was in hers. *There is nothing like a challenge to perk a body up,* she thought happily.

"Starboard tack, Captain!"

His ship was cutting perilously close to her bow as Ross sailed directly across her path.

Startled, she quickly jerked on the mainsheet, loosening the mainsail and spilling air from it. There was nothing she could do but yield; according to the laws of the sea, he had the right of way.

"Better start practicing your 'Aye, aye, sir's,' " he laughed.

The prow of her ship smacked into the turbulence of his wake a bare foot behind the stern of his ship. The letters spelling out *Sea Dreamer* loomed blackly as she slipped by the transom that had so narrowly missed colliding with her vessel.

The boat rocked, bucking like a horse with the impact of his wake.

"You'll need 'em," she heard his shouted voice continuing as his boat sailed on, "when you crew for me in the charter-boat regatta."

"He's dreaming, *Wind Shadow,*" she said to her boat, patting its wheel with as much reassurance as she could muster. "Sea dreaming, all right. We'll never let the jerk take the winner's slot, will we?"

For another few minutes she and Ross Morgan swooped down on each other, playing a mariner's version of chicken. Then they both settled to the serious business of setting up their run for the start. It was a tricky operation, getting up just the right amount of speed. The captain should not build so much speed that the vessel would sail across the start before the gun went off, thus disqualifying the start, and yet also should not sail so slowly that the boat would sacrifice several precious seconds at the start.

"This alone will show who's the better sailor," Alix muttered to herself as she concentrated on the invisible line that was the start. With a small jerk, she hauled in on the mainsheet, whose end was wrapped tightly around her gloved right hand.

Twenty seconds later she was crossing the start line precisely as the starting gun reverberated across the water. Crossing, and cursing.

For Ross Morgan was also crossing that line at the same moment.

Damn you, Ross Morgan. Alix sent the mental curse, along with a few invisible daggers, as she stared over at *Sea Dreamer*. She had wanted to show this chauvinist up from the first instant of the race. Though she knew there were thousands of miles yet before the finish, it had been a matter of pride to outshine him from the very beginning.

Well, he might have foiled her on that score. He was even with her now. But he wasn't going to stay that way. The Bahamas lay upwind, and an unstayed rig could always beat a stayed rig on an upwind course.

"Look out, Morgan," she said softly. "You're about to eat stern spray."

"Wind Shadow calling *Sea Dreamer.* . . .

". . . puts me unquestionably in the lead, Captain Morgan."

"You like being top dog, don't you?"

"Sure I do," Alix answered with hearty conviction. "So do you."

There was a moment of silence. The radio crackled slightly.

"I have to say you're right," he admitted.

"And we're proud of the fact, aren't we, you and I?"

His chuckle sounded clearly. "What's the use of shooting for number two?"

"Exactly." Ross's thought mirrored her own. "You have to aim for perfection. Mediocrity is the refuge of the talentless."

"Whoa. Harsh words." His voice conveyed amusement, but there was also an undertone which seemed to imply he approved.

"Well, much of life is harsh."

She thought of her mother's exhausted face as

the woman would wearily collapse in a chair each evening when she came home. "It's a hard world we have here, and we have to make our way in it. Nobody's offering a free ride. You always pay, one way or another," she said as her thoughts once more returned to the childhood she had spent in poverty. Her mother had tried to succeed but hadn't had the strength. Alix was determined to be stronger—no matter what it took.

"Lady, that sounds a little bitter. You can be hard enough to survive life without having to turn to stone."

"I know." She hesitated a moment, then said, "Look, Ross, I'm not as rigid as I sound."

But, she added silently, *don't you try telling me that "life is as easy as you make it." Sometimes life hurts, and hurts badly. Then a person either sinks under it or fights back.*

"I hear you saying that, but I'm not so sure I believe you. What led you to take such a hard line?"

"Searching for psychological push buttons?" she asked haughtily.

Inside, she was fighting fear and pain. She couldn't reveal to this man the hidden hurts of her life; and yet, for some reason, she actually felt drawn to speak of it with him. That would be crazy, she told herself. She could never trust this overbearing near-stranger.

Still she felt an urge to confide in him. Ruth-

54

lessly she buried the impulse. She needed to keep herself safe, and safety lay in silence.

"Just interested," he answered. "Hey, lady. No big deal. I'm not looking for a soul mate here."

"Good. 'Cause I doubt if you could keep up with me."

Deliberately returning herself—with a silent sigh of relief—to her original topic, she chuckled wickedly.

"In fact, from *Wind Shadow*'s position," she gloated, "I'd say we've *proven* you can't keep up with me."

Lifting the wide-mouthed mug, Ross took a deep draft of coffee, then set the container back down on its even wider base. Within the specially designed sea mug, the café-au-lait surface was slanted, showing that his boat was heeled over, tilted at an angle, and traveling at a good clip.

Not fast enough, though. Somewhere beyond sight, Alix was sailing ahead of him.

It's to be expected, he reminded himself as he settled more comfortably in the cockpit. He'd known all along her boat would pull ahead of his for this portion of the voyage—and that he'd have the advantage on the final leg. But it was hard to stay laid back about it when the competitor was a long, lean blond vixen with a keen mind and a tongue to match.

He reached for the mug again and held it. As his palms heated, the sensation reminded him of the warmth of Alix's skin when he'd held her and kissed her. The very same temperature had radiated from her body.

His mind drifted back to the time they'd shared on that moonless night in the parking lot. Like a favored videotape, he played the memories again and again.

The sleek, soft feel of her lips moving so skillfully against his, the subtle scent floating from her hair, the taste of her velvet mouth as his tongue explored its warm depths. His arm pulling her body tightly into his, and the way her surprising softness fit there. The feel of her strong yet gentle fingers seeking the contours of his back, seeming to drink them in. . . .

A stab of pain brought him back. He saw that he was gripping the mug so tightly that his knuckles were white.

Lord, how he wanted that woman. There were no two ways about it. Though they had not made sleeping together a part of the bet between them, when this race finished he was going to have her. Exactly as he had determined that night in Coconut's. Landfall at St. Thomas would see a double victory for him—a race won and a woman won.

Ross continued to sprawl in the cockpit, one hand reaching out occasionally to make an idle steering correction. His body barely moved. But his mind was fully engaged. Filled with fantasy after fully embellished fantasy of the intriguing, delightful, mind-bendingly sensual ways in which he and Alix could make love.

"Sea Dreamer calling *Wind Shadow*. . . .

". . . and I'll bet you're running your little buns off just maintaining this puny lead of yours."

Alix laughed. "Dream on, Ross. This is like a vacation for me. I've gotten so much rest, I'm positively satiated with it."

"Snuggling up in your lonely bunk, dreaming of me?"

Again she laughed. "You and your ego make a fine pair. I'm sure you're very happy together."

"Well, after our night in the parking lot"—his voice traveled suggestively over the speaker— "I'm sure you know I could make *you* very happy. Ecstatic, in fact."

She hated to admit it to herself, but she was actually enjoying this conversation with Ross. That brash confidence of his was appealing; she'd never been overly fond of wishy-washy types. She was feeling too good to revive the antagonism she had displayed in their first ship-to-ship communication. Besides, she couldn't help savoring a little secret pleasure in the fact that the man wanted her.

"Is this going to be an obscene transmission? Poor, desperate man, ruled by your hormones. You'd better climb out onto your bowsprit and let the ocean spray cool you off."

When his voice came again it had changed. All seriousness, he said, "You know that we responded to each other that night, Alix. There is a very real attraction between us. Let's be adults and admit it."

"Fine. It's true. But it doesn't mean anything."

"Doesn't it?"

"Impulse and action are two very different things. And in this case, they most definitely are going to stay that way."

"Why?"

She didn't answer.

"Why, Alix?"

Perhaps it was the safety of the distance between them, of being able to speak into a mechanical receiver and not have to look into those all-too-mesmerizing blue eyes. Though she'd intended to brush off his question with some simple glib comment, she found herself answering honestly.

"Because you and I are too alike, Ross. Too intense, too driven to be in control. I won't let myself be controlled, even though I don't want a man that *I* can control. I don't believe either of us is capable of relinquishing the reins."

"You mean you don't think we can stop the games, and just let it be what it is, let it happen?"

"That's right. That's the way I see it." She settled into the chair bolted to the floor in front of the communication panel.

She was pleased with the evenness of her tone,

58

its casual air. Honest, but uninvolved. That was the sense she wanted to convey. If her tone was a shield against a deeper involvement with Ross, she managed to hide that fact from herself.

"We have to acknowledge our basic natures," she continued. "I'm proud of my drive, and what I accomplish because of it. But even I can see that that isn't good for personal relationships."

"Sounds more like you don't *have* any personal relationships, romantic ones, that is."

"Not true," she answered a little too quickly. *At least not quite true.*

She pulled up one knee, gripping her left arm around it as she held the speaker in her right hand. The move was a physical response reflecting the unexpected emotional response she'd had to his statement. Why should it hurt to hear him state what she knew was true? After all, it was her choice not to get involved emotionally with the man.

"Of course," she continued, "the problem isn't as difficult for you. Men have always been expected to be dominant in a relationship, and women to be submissive. That's gone on for thousands of years. I'm sure the balance of control has always been in your favor, and thus not a conflict with your nature."

"You think so?" his voice crackled over the transmitter. "Well, to be honest, I'd say that was ninety percent true. But did it ever occur to you that could be boring?"

"Are you kidding? Why do you think I said I don't want a relationship with someone I can control? Of course it's boring, either way, if you've got enough of a mind to see beyond the social constraints laid out for you."

"Interesting that you can see that. So many people can't."

"Mmmm." She made a polite "I'm listening" noise.

But her mind was still digesting his previous statement. So he realized a challenge was necessary in his personal relationships as well. That impressed her. More than one of these blustery, I'm-so-tough kind of guys couldn't tolerate the give and take of a real relationship. They were men who chose mirrors for partners, women who were content merely to stroke the men's overblown yet fragile egos. Now she knew Ross was stronger than that.

Again she felt drawn to him, excited by the prospect of strength matched with strength. But that was emotion talking—her head knew better.

"Of course, you're right about us," he said. "I'd say two or three weeks would be our limit before the power struggle would begin."

"It seems likely, doesn't it?" she agreed.

There. Ross had confirmed her own thoughts. And she wasn't disappointed by that, she assured herself. She wasn't.

"Yep. Even though we'd be fully aware of the pitfalls, we'd probably end up fighting just the same. It would be wonderful, for a while, to find we were meeting a real resistance instead of Jell-O every time we pushed—we'd probably find the experience stimulating beyond belief—but—"

She interrupted. "But ultimately, wonderful as it might be, magical as it might seem to us for a while, it would become a bitter struggle."

"With only one possible winner . . ."

"I know. And I'd hate to crush your ego like that, Ross."

"*My* ego. You'd be the one bleeding in the dust."

"You think so?"

"Lady, I don't want to fracture that self-pro-claimed hard-as-nails psyche of yours, but believe me, Ross Morgan would walk away the victor."

She laughed, loud and long. It was a great release for the tension. Ross and she were in perfect agreement on the disaster that a relationship would be. Stopping her laughter at last, she demanded, "See? See? We can't even discuss a relationship without trying to one-up each other on who would end it!"

"Well, there's something I *can* end, and that's this transmission. It's time for me to check in with Tully. Take care, my favorite iron maiden."

With a mutual chuckle they signed off.

Whuufff.

The down pillow protested the pummeling that Alix was giving it.

61

Darn, it was difficult to sleep during the day. Jamming her head back into her fluffed-beyond-recognition pillow, she forced her eyes shut.

Now, relax, she ordered herself. *You know you'll need to be awake tonight to keep watch.* Nighttime. That was the dangerous time for single-handers. In the dark one could be rammed by a freighter before one realized it was there.

Even if their watch happened to see you, those massive phantoms couldn't change course soon enough to avoid disaster. It was the small ship's responsibility to look out for its own safety. That meant keeping a sharp eye out, and you couldn't do that if your eyes were closed.

The trouble at the moment was that Alix was not the least bit sleepy. It wasn't overconcern for her boat. The self-steering mechanism was set and working beautifully. Her radar would warn of any object approaching; in the daylight, she had plenty of leeway for maneuvering as soon as the warning buzzer alerted her.

The problem was partly the damned daylight —a whole oceanful of brilliant sunshine. But mostly the problem was Ross.

She couldn't get the man off her mind. Every time she closed her eyes she saw him. As *Wind Shadow* rose and fell rhythmically she found herself picturing his lips against hers, imagining his arms around her.

Lord, the man had turned her on! Who would have thought a simple chemical response could be so powerful? It had been days since he'd so much as touched her, yet just thinking of it made her ache to be in his embrace.

This was ridiculous! Utterly ridiculous. She was starting to look forward to arriving at St. Thomas as much to see him in the flesh as to the pleasure of winning the race.

Of course becoming a couple was out of the question. But, she suddenly wondered, did that really have to rule out lovemaking?

Alix's eyes popped open again. She pondered the possibility in depth as she stared at the polished teak ceiling above her berth.

Actually, she mused, it was entirely feasible. Making love to a man once or twice didn't necessarily mean a woman was committed to him. In this case it would simply satisfy a craving that would disappear as soon as her "appetite" had been satisfied. She and Ross were mature adults, after all. From their conversation over the radiophone, it was clear they both understood the terms of this situation, and all the ramifications.

So what could be the harm in answering this one question hovering between them?

"Wind Shadow calling *Sea Dreamer*. . . .

". . . so comparing my noon fix with yours, Ross, I'd say you're falling solidly behind."

"Early days yet, my girl."

"Don't count too heavily on making it all up on that last leg, fella. You'll have the advantage there, it's true, but *Wind Shadow* is a real thoroughbred. When she takes a lead she holds it."

"Just like her captain, eh?"

"You bet."

"I'm sure you'll give me a good run for my money. And we couldn't have asked for better weather for this race, could we?"

"It's a sailor's dream," she agreed.

"Speaking of that, this sailor's been having some dreams of his own. . . ."

Even through the mild interference of the radiophone transmission, Ross's husky intonation was enough to stir her libido. The more he talked, the more she could feel her body respond.

"Reckless dreams, wanton dreams. I'm sure you can imagine."

"Yes," she answered quietly. "I can imagine."

And she could. All too well. She had only to recall her own dreams, both waking and sleeping.

"I was thinking. I'm confident we can be good sports about this race when it finishes, Alexandra. You know, shake hands"—his voice caressed the words—"smile, give the winner a heartfelt victory kiss."

"Mmm-hmmm." Alix was contemplating much more than just a kiss. But then, she knew Ross was implying much more than just a kiss.

The two of them had talked a good deal over these past few days. The ostensible purpose had been reporting their positions and status to one another, but much more had been exchanged.

Somehow the distance that radiophone communication provided—the freedom from having to deal with one another's physical presence—had allowed her and Ross to mellow their competitive, sophisticated repartee. It had been interspersed with a more human, sharing type of dialogue.

Yet the sharing they really wanted was on a physical, sensual level.

What would she lose if she chose to make love with Ross Morgan? The satisfaction of rejecting him seemed to be the only credit on the "no lovemaking" side of the ledger. Balancing it—possibly outweighing it—would be the pleasure of sharing Ross's bed.

She could, of course, wonder if he was a good lover. But the evidence of the kissing and caressing that night at Coconut's pointed to the man being a very good lover indeed. It was, she told herself, a good bet. So maybe she—

"*Wind Shadow. Wind Shadow.* Hey, my iron butterfly, have we been cut off? Come back if you're still there."

"I'm here, all right, Ross. Here, and miles ahead of you."

Miles ahead of you, indeed. Ross Morgan didn't know it yet, but the seduction of Alexandra Boudreaux was no longer in his hands.

She grinned at the metal receiver snugged into her palm. Just winning the race was no longer enough. The captain of *Wind Shadow* had herself a new goal.

CHAPTER FIVE

"Aarggh!"

Alix threw her pencil down in disgust. She stared at the course that she'd just finished plotting.

One hundred and twelve miles in twenty-four hours.

Great. But how many miles had Ross covered during the same time? She had no idea. What she *did* know was that it would be more miles than she had sailed.

Hands clamped on the arms of the chair, she shoved herself out of it. How could she be losing her hard-fought lead barely halfway through the race?

They weren't even out of the Bahamas yet. In fact, she thought as she stomped her way up the companionway and into the cockpit, it was the Bahamas that was snatching her sweet head start right out of her rope-burned fingers.

With an entirely unfriendly expression, she stared at the long dark smudge that corrupted the western horizon.

"Eleuthera, your name may mean *freedom* in Greek, but you sure don't mean freedom to me," she shouted at the island.

A fledgling norther was already making things difficult. Winds were blowing from the southeast. Alix knew they would work their way around just like the hands of a clock. They'd be back in the east by the time the storm blew itself out. Right now the rising southeasterly wind was making for some hard sailing as she and Ross fought to keep from being blown onto Eleuthera's coral-strewn northwestern shore.

"I hate sailing hard to weather," she groused as she released the self-steering and took control of the wheel.

She had good reason to be upset. She knew that Ross's boat handled better under these conditions than hers did. She was having difficulty holding her course; he wasn't.

That meant *Sea Dreamer* was moving faster. Which wouldn't have been great, but would have been tolerable, *if* she had maintained the wide gap between them. But her solid lead had been eroding all day yesterday. And far too much of today had been spent avoiding a too close encounter with Eleuthera, as would tonight.

"Oh, damn!" she burst out in a fine show of patience. "Hellfire and damnation!"

"Come on. Blow, baby, blow!"
Ross threw back his silver head and laughed.

"I don't want a measly fifteen knots," he called up to the still-blue sky, "I want to see some real wind here!"

Huge white clouds raced across the expanse of brilliant blue, and Ross raced with them crest and trough. Whitecaps laughed across the billowing waves, and Ross laughed right along with them.

"Think you're so far ahead you can't be caught, eh, Captain Boudreaux?" he asked aloud. "Well, lady, I'm coming up fast on the inside."

Yes, sir, this fortunate little norther was going to blow him right into the lead.

It had handed him a potent weapon—the male's superior strength. He would use that advantage shamelessly to push his vessel to her structural limits in the high winds.

Bracing himself for the sudden jolt, he released the mainsheet and took the full force of the boom's pull in his arms and shoulders. Carefully he paid out a few inches of rope, then reveled in the sudden kick as *Sea Dreamer*'s mainsail caught the extra wind and leapt forward, heeled to a dramatic angle. Sea spray smacked his face as the ship sliced through the growing waves.

"Man," he laughed, "I'm surfing now. I'm really wailing."

Deep-blue eyes searched the turbulent sky. This storm was going to take a full two days to blow out. There would be some very heavy weather, and a serious confrontation between man and nature.

He felt a familiar thrill of anticipation at the challenge. This time the rewards of winning would be even sweeter. Though his body would pay dearly for the abuse he would give it, the delight of besting Alix should more than compensate. For Ross a little discomfort could never outweigh the pleasure of proving himself.

The heavy creakings of the boat's rigging as it met the force of the wind was music to his ears. *Sea Dreamer* was living up to her name, she was making a dream of a sail.

"Enjoy your last few hours out in front, Alexandra," he shouted into the wind. "Because you won't be seeing the race from *that* position again."

". . . would say, Alix my sweet, that leaves you firmly in second—or should I say last?—place."

"What was that phrase you used so recently? *Early days,* I think it was. Take those words to heart, Ross. And prepare that monumental ego of yours to handle a little disappointment. Because it's coming your way!"

"Ah," he laughed, and the resonance of that laugh sent her blood pressure rising two points, "but *my* vessel is a real thoroughbred. When she takes a lead she keeps it. Of course," he confided, "we know that phrase has been bandied around lately, used as an easy bit of bragging. This time, though, there's a difference."

His voice stopped. It left a deep silence broken only by the occasional crackle of interference.

"This time," he stated, "it's true."

"My English grandmother," she tossed back, "had a saying that fits here. 'Time will tell its own tale.' In other words, 'It ain't over till it's over.'"

"There are certain moments in history when an event occurs that makes inevitable the chain of events that follows, Captain Alix. This lead of mine is one of them."

Her gasp of amused disbelief sounded clearly in the small cabin. The man's ego was truly beyond measure. Either that or he was putting her on with a subtlety and skill that, if captured on film, could earn him an Academy Award.

"You have the gall to think of your puny little lead in a race as a turning point in *history?* Come on, guy. Are you drunk, or what?"

"Who, me?"

"Too innocent, sailor. Admit it. You're pushing yourself to the limit—it's the only way you could eke out a lead against me—"

"Oh ho. Who's got an ego problem then?"

"—and I'll bet," she continued without the slightest acknowledgment of his interruption, "that you've been popping caffeine pills in order to sail straight through. It's no wonder your mind's become warped. Sleep deprivation does strange things to the brain. And when the brain is pretty strange to *begin* with . . ."

"Oh, you're admitting I have a brain? Hallelujah, praise the saints."

She noticed that Ross didn't deny her guess about the caffeine tablets. She'd known that the odds were good he was artificially extending his hours to exploit this norther. Truth was, she was tempted to take the stimulant herself but unwilling to risk the aftereffects—the grainy head, the dragged-out feeling that came from squandering her body's reserves.

No, she would need all her energy for the end of the race. For this man to abuse himself now, he must really believe that he could gain such an impressive lead on her during the hard-blowing storm that he could afford to coast for a while afterward, while he recuperated.

Go ahead, buddy. Count on it. You'll find it to be a fatal error to make assumptions about Alexandra Boudreaux, she thought, her lips set in a grim line.

"If you have nothing further to report . . ."

Besides the fact you're already past San Salvador and I haven't reached it yet, she completed with silent, sardonic disgust. What a landmark. San Salvador Island, where Columbus found America—and she lost her lead.

"No, Captain Boudreaux. Just some really honkin' speed out of *Sea Dreamer.*"

"I'm not exactly coasting myself," she replied dryly. But her boast sounded hollow. They both knew that she was moving at least a knot slower than he was.

"Really? Just the same, I suggest you start warming up for that victory kiss. I'm going to take great pleasure in collecting it, I assure you, sweet, *sweet* Alexandra."

Ten minutes later, Alix was still fuming.

Victory kiss, my Aunt Fanny, she thought. A kiss was all he was ever going to get. How could she have even *considered* going to bed with this idiot, this braggart, this swaggering little pirate?

She could thank her lucky stars that he had no idea she'd contemplated making love to him.

Temporary insanity. That's what it had been, temporary insanity. For the tenth time she told herself that as she huddled before the wheel, the salt spray drizzling down her sunburned face and onto her bright-blue foul-weather gear.

So what if the man had a touch that felt like the most natural, most "right" touch in the world? That was only physical. In all other respects, he was repugnant to her. So what if he was diabolically good-looking? That was only his outer form, a casing, a shell. It was nothing. So what if he was a fine sailor who could press even someone as good as herself to the point where it hurt? That was only . . . only . . .

She sighed. Talent. That was *talent.*

But it still didn't make him a person of good character. It was certainly no reason to trust him with intimacy. Now if he could just get past that massive ego of his, *then* there might be someone worth knowing.

Regret washed a corner of her soul. Despite the fact that the man's braggadocio made him infuriating to deal with, and despite the knee-jerk anger it provoked in her, she knew somewhere inside him was a strong, intelligent man who would make a marvelous lover. And though she wanted to know that lover, she could not afford to subvert her life for the months it would take to break through to him. She would have to regard it as another one of those sad realities that life seemed to delight in dealing out . . . and move on.

She tightened her grip on the wheel even farther. Unable to find a positive point in the situation, she turned her attention to an equally aggravating question. Why couldn't this cursed norther shift into the southern portion of its cycle?

She *needed* the wind to blow from the south. Then the *Wind Shadow* would show some razzle-dazzle again, and she could climb right up Ross's rudder. Every hour the wind remained in the southeast was another league the man gained on her.

"Come on, Mother Nature," she hollered at the huge rolling waves, "let's show a little *solidarity* here!"

It was two hours late in coming, but Alix finally got her wish. Heeding her frustrated plea, the wind veered abruptly to the south.

With a huge sigh of relief, Alix tacked offshore, pushing the little vessel for everything it had. She was on her way again, and the storm's driving force would have *Wind Shadow* eating up Ross's lead with each passing hour.

She knew that, Mother Nature knew that—but Ross wasn't going to know it.

Let that king-sized ego of his stay nice and cozy, all wrapped up in a false sense of security, she chortled to herself. The pleasure of zapping him with the news would be all the greater. After all, the wind shift probably hadn't hit him yet. He'd still be thinking she was pinching along. It was entirely possible that she and the new wind would arrive simultaneously.

A truly wicked chuckle emerged from her throat. As she watched her own wake vanish behind her, it grew and grew until it was an outright laugh.

The laugh was replaced by crocodile tears when she placed her next call to *Sea Dreamer*.

"These crazy winds," she complained to Ross. "If this storm would start acting the way it's supposed to, instead of loitering in the southeast, I'd be showing you some real sailing instead of poking along back here."

"So you've taken to blaming the winds, have you, poor woman? Why don't you just sit down and make a list of all your excuses for why you're not as good a sailor as me?"

"It'd serve you right if the winds blew you straight into the Silver Banks."

"I'll bet you'd like to see me smashed up on some coral head right about now, wouldn't you?" he laughed. "Sorry, baby. I'm a darned sight better navigator than that. You'd better hope you are too."

"There's no way I'd blunder into the Silver Banks and you know it. All you have to do is sail due east to avoid them."

"I'll just write that down. I might forget, you know. The way *Sea Dreamer* is flying, I—"

"Ross," she interrupted. "I'm in no mood."

There, she thought. *That sounds testy enough. It ought to make him believe I'm still crawling and thoroughly steamed about the whole deal.*

As Ross talked on, this time about his galley and the "superior" techniques he had developed for cooking while a boat was surging along at eight knots, she thought, *Now here's a nice change to bring on that old song—I'm crying on the outside, laughing on the inside.*

Ah, what a delight it was to fool him this way. Pure pleasure. She shook her head in wonder at her earlier lapse of sanity. Share the intimacies of the bedroom with this fellow? She wasn't even going to give him an accurate position fix from now on.

"I suppose you're just wailing along," she sniffed, interrupting his cheerful flow of chatter.

Lounging back in her chair, she congratulated herself on how well that simple sentence had conveyed the demoralized tone of one resigned to defeat and simultaneously disgusted by it. If she didn't know better, she'd believe herself!

"Now, Alix. Don't rub salt in your own wounds. I'll tell you what. Why don't we agree that we just won't talk about my incredible lead anymore?"

Twenty-four hours, Ross, my boy. Go ahead and gloat for twenty-four hours. Then we'll have a real race again. And forty-eight hours after that, you'll be on your knees.

Bucking like a pain-crazed bronco, *Sea Dreamer* plunged down the side of a huge wave. The shriek of the twenty-knot wind as it tore through the rigging was the constant, keening wail of a banshee.

That wind was shifting quickly now. First it had veered to the south, and now it was blowing out of the west. Ross stared into the wildly whipping ocean, marveling for the thousandth time at the way the wind ripped the tops right off the huge, undulating waves. Despite the atmospheric fury, there wasn't a single reef in his sails.

He still had no doubt he could power this thing through. All it took was guts and stamina and determination, fast reflexes and fast thinking—all of which he had in spades. An open-seas storm was no place for false modesty. You had to know your strengths, and follow your instincts. And right now they dictated a mid-course correction.

Fifteen minutes later, Ross felt enough in control to call and report his tack to Alix. In fact, he had started to consider taking in just one reef to make it a little easier on *Sea Dreamer*.

Not that he wasn't still strong enough to keep pushing, he told himself. But with so much ocean behind him, he didn't need to abuse his boat—or himself—to this extent. Even with a reef in his mainsail, he'd be handily pulling ahead of Alix. The new wind would not have reached her yet, way back where she undoubtably was.

As his thick boots clattered down the companionway he couldn't stifle the grin that broke out on his spray-crusted face. She was just going to *love* hearing about the time he was making now.

"Oh, you just tacked, did you?" was her rejoinder, uttered with a particularly self-satisfied chuckle.

"Well, Ross, old salt, *I* tacked hours ago."

"What?"

That sneaky witch. She'd been lying to him. Leading him on. Ross nearly slammed down the receiver. If she'd tacked hours ago, it meant the wind change had hit her well before she'd fed him that moan-and-groan bull about pinching into the wind. She'd been riding hot and heavy on his tail and he hadn't suspected a thing.

77

He felt the anger flood over him like thick molten lava. Outmaneuvered. *Him,* outmaneuvered. Nobody bested Ross Morgan.

"And I suppose you're running without reefs?"

"You don't remember very well, do you?" she asked with appalling good humor. "I told you when we first debated this subject that I reef when it finally becomes necessary. Usually all I need is one reef to pull in one sail—like this time."

"Per sail, and you're running wing and wing."

"Right. And running very well, I might add. Care to compare speeds?"

Lady, what I want to do right now, you don't want to know.

"Don't bother. You won't be sighting me any time soon."·

"Won't I?"

Her silvery peal of laughter just before she ended the transmission echoed in Ross's ears a long, long time.

It stayed with him as he felt the wind roar out of the northwest at twenty-five knots. It stayed with him as his body began protesting the punishment he continued to deal it.

He needed to rest; his muscles, his aching head cried out for respite. His mind, too, was protesting—he was too experienced a sailor not to realize he was risking his health, his vessel, and quite possibly his life in this insane drive to best her.

But his pride overruled it all. For Alix to regain the superior position in this race was unthinkable. No way was that hell-bent sea nymph going to catch up with him.

Determination became coupled with action; Ross continued to press *Sea Dreamer* to her utmost limit. The wind was now barreling in from the northwest, and Ross belayed his mainsail fully out on one side and spread his huge genoa sail out on the other, wing and winging it just as Alix was doing miles behind him.

Still he ran with no reefs—like the cry "No prisoners!" the phrase "No reefs!" rang in his head—and as he sailed he kept thinking, *I ought to rig a preventer.*

But to carry that action out he would have to leave the helm, and he couldn't do that. His hands were full driving the ship.

Besides, he told himself as he thought for the fifth time about the preventer, *I'm making fantastic speed.*

He was. *Sea Dreamer* was surfing in a building sea. Racing along at nine knots per hour. It was dynamite, absolute dynamite.

Ten hours later it was pure nitroglycerine—fission power—fusion power—as he stampeded over the waves. The wind was up to thirty-five knots, gale force, and the seas were running at seven to ten feet, looking like foothills gone crazy with Saint Vitus' Dance.

Not a single reef point was tied. The sails were

still—in the midst of the whipping rain and wind —fully extended. Charged with the last of the caffeine tablets, Ross was on a triple-header adrenaline high. It was built equally from the stimulant, the grandeur of the storm, and the wild speed of *Sea Dreamer*. The vessel was making absolutely unheard-of speeds, at times hitting thirteen-knot surges.

"Nobody would believe it," he shouted into the howling wind, wishing for the first time that he had someone else on board, some crew member who could verify this record-breaking progress.

At that particular moment there wasn't a shred of doubt in Ross's mind who was the better sailor. He was convinced Alix couldn't handle the helm that was under his command right now. Hell, three-quarters of his peers from Fort Lauderdale to Barbados couldn't handle it.

His hands, almost white from the strain of manhandling the steering for hour after hour, clutched the wheel in a death grip. The wild spray was almost blinding him; every muscle in his body ached and his head pounded. But still he laughed into the fury of the storm.

It was wild and savage and beautiful. Not unlike Alexandra Boudreaux.

Disjointed images of Alexandra began to dance in his mind. The fire in her eyes as she argued a point with him, the glow of her curling blond hair as the lounge's light caught in their tumbling, sun-streaked mass. That slick, sensual trail her thumb had followed on the glass. . . .

Now *there* was an unconscious display of sensuality. Though the woman hadn't realized it, that slow repetitive motion had been a blatant announcement to him that she was deeply connected to the sensual side of her nature, responsive to stimuli in a way that few other women were.

Oh no, she wouldn't be getting away with a mere victory kiss in St. Thomas, he told himself as he wiped salt water from his red-rimmed eyes.

Braced into almost stonelike stillness against the wheel, Ross found himself recalling in cherishing, lingering detail every nuance of the two kisses they had shared. The thought of her lips, the feel of her lips, the taste of her lips began to dominate his reflections. That last kiss in particular had told him that Alix was a woman who could be stirred by the right touch, drawn from one level of intimacy to the next and the next. A man who could awaken those warm, waiting responses, a man of experience and subtlety, could give this woman the kind of pleasure that she deserved, that she clearly needed.

Her soft, sleekly curved neck, yielding beneath the workings of his lips and tongue, responding with a quiver to the tiny, tugging little bites of his teeth, warm and—

With a jerk, Ross found himself staring at the mast ahead.

Damn. He'd almost fallen asleep. And no more caffeine tablets to fight the drowsiness.

You should ease up, a part of him whispered seductively. *Enough. You need to rest. Reef the sails. Then heave-to, and ride out the storm. You have the lead. Make it easy on yourself.*

But even as his mind filled with images of "shutting down" the boat and crawling into the bunk that hadn't been slept in for such a long, long time, his hands remained welded to the wheel.

Still the thought of rest became more and more seductive.

At first he rejected the idea out of hand. Look at the speed he was making. At this rate Alix would end up so far behind it wouldn't even be a race anymore. But as the passing time took its toll, he began to warm to the idea of compromise. Finally his ego struck a bargain with his exhausted body—two more hours of driving his boat to her limit and then he would reef. Reef, and rest.

Relaxing his two-fisted grip on the wheel for an instant, he raised one hand to wipe the salt water from his face. Where was Alix at this moment? How far back in the storm was she, and how was she faring?

A mental picture of her at her helm, zipping past him as the Florida sun shone on her gleaming blond hair, suddenly clouded his mind. Then he imagined her pulling in her mainsheet with a practiced move, one well-shaped leg braced against the steering column.

One thing he couldn't deny was that the woman was a fine sailor. The way she'd assumed the lead in the start of the race, the way she'd held on to it for so long, even that trick of hers in making a bid to regain it were all hallmarks of a first-rate skipper.

Amazing that the talent came in such a beautiful package. Alix's face floated before him again, all shades of gold. Smooth golden skin, shining hair of palest gold, lips of honey-gold, parting in a soft smi—

Cra-a-ack!

Reality rushed in upon Ross like an avalanche. Wild lights exploded in his brain. He was awake —totally awake, with the pain of a badly barked elbow shooting straight up his arm into his skull.

Around him the whole world was an oblique kaleidoscope of raging water and sails tilted at impossible angles.

He was falling. Vertigo claimed his head and stomach. He didn't know if he was falling down or up. His body was shaking, demanding action. Adrenaline pumped until he was quivering. But his eyes were still sending his brain insane images. And his body knew it was falling.

Instinctively, even as he tumbled, he latched onto safety, catching an arm around the solid barrel of one of the winches, tangling his legs in his safety line. Stunned into immobility, he clung to the winch as his eyes focused on a wall of black ocean raging toward him.

It took a second for his sleep-fuzzed mind to reorient itself. Then Ross realized that *Sea Dreamer* was turned sideways, plunging broadside down a monstrous wave like a locomotive on a one-way track to annihilation.

CHAPTER SIX

Alix fought the last two reef points, struggling to get the second reef in her main secured. Three battle-weary minutes later, she had subdued the frenzied sail. This was heavy weather indeed, she reflected, to require two reefs from *her* boat.

Another minute more she stayed where she was, holding on to the deckhouse, feeling *Wind Shadow* pitching beneath her as she caught her breath. Then she carefully crawled along the water-sluiced deck, dragging her lifeline, until she regained the helm.

She released the wheel to her control and wedged herself into position. This gale was putting a king-sized crimp into her racing style. The only consolation was that Ross was suffering through it right along with her. The focus had shifted. Instead of making headway, the two of them had to worry about just plain making it through the storm.

Not that it was the worst storm she'd ever sailed through, Alix reminded herself. She'd dealt with some incredibly heavy seas. But that fact didn't win a yachtsman any prizes, beyond living to tell of it. She had no doubt the same was true for Ross.

Ross. It had been a long time since she'd spoken with him. Hours longer than the usual break between radiophone contacts. She felt a real desire to call him. To hear his voice, reassure herself that he was doing okay, to let him know how she was coping.

Alix fought the impulse. There was no need to feel that way. It was a dependency, a weakness. A strong woman like herself stayed strong by resisting such clinging impulses.

You don't need to speak with him, she ordered herself. *You don't.*

But still she longed to hear his voice, felt compelled to speak with him. She almost felt as if by calling she would guarantee everything would be fine and that if she didn't call something awful might happen.

"I think the isolation is starting to get to you, Alix my girl," she warned herself. "You're starting to invent things to justify getting on that radiophone."

What was she doing? she asked herself in disgust. To call "just to see if you're all right" was such a lame excuse.

So why couldn't she stop wanting, needing to hear his voice? Why was she trying to find excuses to communicate with Ross? She knew damn well it was more than loneliness. She cared about him, cared about him as a woman cares for a man.

She had taken a personal interest in his welfare, Alix admitted to herself. And that disturbed her. She didn't want to have such a concern for him. She didn't want to care. It led only to heartbreak, as her mother's experience so clearly showed. She had to ignore this ridiculous feeling that something was wrong.

"The man is fine," she told the turbulent waves, as if speaking the words out loud gave them more truth.

"He's an excellent sailor. And he's probably handling this norther better than you are. So stop worrying."

She wedged herself tighter into her helm position, using her feet to brace against the steering column and lock her body in its seat. She stared at the wickedly wailing winds.

"You fool. Ross Morgan is probably thumbing his nose at the storm right this very minute."

Ross clung for dear life to the winch.

The wheel was continuing to spin wildly. *Sea Dreamer* was sliding at breakneck speed toward the bottom of a huge wave. And above and behind Ross towered a house-high wall of angry ocean.

Though he had a death grip on the winch, his sailor's mind was skipping right past the fear of the moment, calculating the speed at which *Sea*

Dreamer was plunging. More than fifteen knots, it was clear. Just as clear was an inevitable conclusion. She was going to slam sideways with the wave.

An instant later he had his prediction confirmed as the boat crashed into the trough of the wave.

She was broadside to the wind, rolling wildly. With tremendous force the boom whipped across the boat, and as the boat shuddered at the impact, finished with the sickening crunch of splintering timber. The noise was accompanied by the softer but equally distressing sound of canvas ripping.

Beneath the deck, Ross heard a gurgling rush of water. The sound could only be seawater spewing in through broken ports.

For an awful moment Ross stared at what had once been his beautiful ship. The sail and boom flapped piteously in the wind, like the broken wing of a wild bird. *Sea Dreamer*'s pain was his own. He felt every wound.

Forcing his mind to function as logically and unemotionally as possible, he tore his eyes from the sail and worked his way back to the wheel. The waves were breaking over the deck, roaring their defiance. Every instant he had to be alert for a wild slap of water that could knock him unconscious. Little good his safety harness would do him then.

When he was securely settled at the helm, he

ticked off the damage. The main was ripped. The boom was broken. The jib was stuck to leeward. The rudder was jammed and guiding him in circles. Portlights were smashed out, and most important, the waves hitting the side of the boat were washing quantities of seawater in through those broken ports.

Clearly his first action had to be to get the boat turned so that his broken portlights were upwind. Then he could seal them off from the sea and stop the ship from filling with water and giving him a one-way ticket to Davy Jones's locker.

The next half hour was a nightmare of battling the elements and his wounded ship as Ross fought to save *Sea Dreamer* and himself.

He got his jib rolled in, then he stripped the pole and stowed it. Though it killed him to listen to the sound, he hung his ripped sail like a wind vane, where it proceeded to beat itself to death in the wind. That gave him breathing space to survey the damage.

He checked the rudder and found that it was, as he had suspected, stuck. It was steering him to port, so he lay ahull and took down the main to ride out the storm.

Well, for the moment he had saved his ship. Now he faced the most difficult task of all. He had to call Alix and relay the whole humiliating story.

She would know, she would *know* that it had happened from his own stupid determination to power through the storm. The woman was going to laugh herself silly. Even if she had enough good taste not to do it in his hearing, he knew she would burst with delight when she learned of his disaster.

His boots landed heavily on each step as he climbed down into the cabin. When he reached it the seawater sloshed nearly up to his knees. Thankful that his communication equipment was behind a glass door and had not been put out of commission by salt water, Ross sank into the chair before the radio. He was exhausted.

The adrenaline rush that had hit him at the same moment as the disaster had awakened him now took its toll, and he found his muscles shaking, his stomach churning. He did his best to fight the sensation and managed to hold it at bay until it stabilized.

He opened the glass door. A quick check showed him that he had barely enough juice to transmit.

The boat's motor was dead, a victim of the salt water that flooded the cabin, with hardly enough amperage left to run a flashlight, let alone an engine. Without the engine he couldn't generate more power. The power he *had* wasn't adequate, but it was going to have to do.

For a moment he made no motion to call. Depression weighed as heavily on him as his sea-soaked clothes. He had to call Alix, yet his ego cringed from the impending humiliation.

Damn. Damn, damn, damn. The rudder problem was severe. He couldn't count on his emergency tiller to do the job. He *had* to ask for her to come—even to himself, he couldn't say the word *rescue*—to come stand by to "assist" him. In this empty stretch of ocean there was no one else to call on.

With as decisive a motion as his bone-weary body could muster, Ross reached for the mike.

". . . rudder broken and . . . boom's in the same sha . . . across the . . . running bare poles, seem to be stable at . . ."

Alix struggled to hear Ross's transmission. His power was so low, it kept breaking up.

"Ross, do you need me there?"

The crackle of interference went on for what seemed forever.

"Repeating—Ross, do you need my help?"

At last came back a faint, "If you like."

Then she clearly heard a huge sigh. "Damn it, the truth is yes. I need your help, Alix."

Knowing what it would cost her to say that to him, Alix understood completely what it was doing to the pride of the man, alone in his ravaged boat twenty-five miles away, to make that admission.

"Right," she replied crisply.

She did not even consider adding to that. Not by one single gloating word. The time for one-upmanship between them was past. Ross was in a serious predicament. She had to do anything she could to help.

As she listened, she felt her stomach roiling, her fingers turning cold against the receiver. He'd said nothing about his own physical condition. Was he hurt, and too proud to say so? She didn't think so—it was the transmission that was weak, she noted, his voice was as strong as ever. But she wanted so much to confirm it. To see him this very moment. To throw her arms around him.

Back off, girl, back off, she warned herself. You are misreading your own reaction. This emotion you feel is just concern for a man in trouble, not concern for a loved one.

But Ross needed help. She couldn't waste time sitting here analyzing her motivations.

"I have your position," she transmitted. "I estimate between five and six hours to reach you. Can you maintain?"

". . . think so. I may need to put in . . . emergency tiller . . . to check it out. Damn, Alix, if this boat were a horse, I'd shoot it straight between the eyes and put it out of its misery."

If ever she had heard a voice that was laughing so it wouldn't cry, she thought, it seemed to her Ross's voice was it just then.

"She's got a good skipper," Alix radioed back. That was all she'd intended to say, but suddenly she found herself speaking again, her voice almost husky.

"*Sea Dreamer* will pull through this and be flying proud again. I'm sure of it. You'll make sure of it."

"Thank you for that, Alix. I'll . . . when you . . ."

The rest of his transmission was lost in a burst of interference. When it didn't improve, she ended transmission.

She walked away from the receiver carrying a warm, protective feeling for Ross.

The man wasn't so bad. He'd swallowed enough of that massive pride of his to ask for her help. That was a positive sign. Maybe there was hope, after all. She found herself contemplating her impending victory kiss in a new light. Perhaps she would give him more than a simple congratulatory buss on the cheek, after all. . . .

As she set course for her rescue mission, the warm feeling for Ross continued. And while she sat at the wheel she found her mind occupying the time with an intriguing variety of daydreams whose only common thread was that they started with a victory kiss and that sensuality played a prime role.

Alix's new fantasies and her good feelings toward Ross managed to survive for nearly an hour.

After that there was a slow erosion. Though the storm was abating, it wasn't over yet. To reach *Wind Shadow* she was having to sail a difficult, cold, and wet course. The wind was howling. It was a forty-eight-degree wind, damned cold even with her foul-weather gear—even if she hadn't been sailing with the wind and waves at her back, splashing her with icy thoroughness. She was slightly ahead of beam on the starboard side, reaching fast, but big seas were slamming into her from the side.

It was a nonstop cold shower, and it was more than effective in cooling off her feelings for him. Kindliness turned into annoyance. After all, if the man hadn't been grandstanding, playing macho games to try and show her up, he would never have landed in this mess, and she wouldn't have to be freezing to death trying to save him from it.

"Well, buddy, you did it this time, didn't you?" Ross said aloud.

He stared down at his "handiwork." In this case, the rudder housing.

"Your rudder cable is broken, hotshot. *And* your quadrant is absolutely pretzeled from being forced past the stop."

No question about it. It was emergency tiller time.

A few minutes later, he was ready to install the piece. He unscrewed the deck plate and fitted the replacement to the top of the rudder post. It was difficult to move, but he managed it.

Now he could bring the boat around. With the waves still breaking over him, he began. Things were looking better, he thought, pleased with himself. He stayed pleased for a whole fifteen seconds. On the sixteenth he felt the sponginess in the tiller. The sensation brought the hairs on the back of his neck to full attention.

Without thinking, he released his hold on the malfunctioning tiller for an instant, then replaced his hand. It was as though some part of him believed a new grip would magically cure the problem.

I didn't feel any sponginess here. I only thought I did, he told himself, as if the words were a charm that would make his thought truth. He held his breath, then worked the steering back and forth.

This time there was no doubt. The response was spongy.

Ross felt his heart sink. "I'm in big trouble here. Big trouble."

His steering was, in fact, next to nonexistent. Yet he had to get the boat turned around somehow. Until he could get those broken ports away from those heavy-hitting waves, she would keep taking on water. Bailing would be useless, and he and *Sea Dreamer* could end up as nothing but a memory and a little patch of foam on the waves.

That frightening thought spurred Ross on. In record time he had his mainsail back up. Though the boom was broken it would serve, allowing him to use the wind's force upon it for steering power. And that was precisely what he did, jibing through the eye of the wind. He could not help wincing as the sail, attached to its broken boom, flopped across and crashed once more. But at least the wind was finally portside.

As Ross contemplated his next action, he had a morbid flash of the headline it would probably generate somewhere in the back pages of the sailing magazines:

"Charter Captain Lost at Sea. Ross Morgan Drowns While Diving to Repair Rudder."

Well, there was no use debating the pros and cons of the issue. He had only himself to depend on. He had to do it.

Without further reflection, Ross hauled himself up the companionway.

Taking a well-secured line, he tied the other end around his wrist. Then he took in a tremendous breath and dove off the stern of the wildly rocking boat.

Almost instantly the boat rolled over him as he descended through the turbulent water.

It brought with it a terrifying sight. The fiberglass of the rudder had shattered, torn loose from the metal post that was its center. Huge glass-sharp shreds of fiberglass were stabbing toward him with each erratic motion of the boat above.

He was trapped.

A fear colder than the water hit him as he realized he needed to get back to the surface . . . and couldn't. With the boat washing over him, he must instead dive deeper, down below the dagger-sharp shards.

Though his lungs were starting to burst with a need for air, Ross battled his body's instincts to rise, and kicked himself deeper. He fought his way under the deadly rudder, twice catching a sharp jab into his legs.

As he came back up well away from the shattered fiberglass, the side of the boat lurched forward and slammed into his shoulder.

Using the rope, he hauled himself hand over hand up it to regain the deck of the boat, teeth gritted against the pain in his shoulder.

He collapsed on deck. A trickle of blood joined the rivulets of salt water draining down his legs.

Sea Dreamer was doomed. And he wasn't far behind.

The rudder was barely functional at the moment. It would only get worse. The remaining fiberglass would be slowly torn away by the heavy action of the sea until nothing was left but the post. Then he would have no steering at all.

Ross's mind totaled the damages inflicted on *Sea Dreamer*. She was now a pitiful, smashed shell of her former self. And for what?

Like a knell of doom, one word came back to him. It echoed in his mind, rolling there in the soft, silvery tones of Alexandra Boudreaux. Echoed, over and over again.

Hubris.

CHAPTER SEVEN

As Alix bore down on the boat, the sight of *Sea Dreamer* was both a welcome and a depressing one. Welcome, because it was still afloat and was a tangible symbol that she would be seeing another human being after days and days of isolation. Depressing, because the once beautiful vessel was so bedraggled.

Sea Dreamer had obviously taken on a great deal of water. She was riding very low, lumbering through the swells. Her mainsail—if that tattered rag could be called a sail at all—drooped from the mast as though it were ashamed of itself. The boat's erratic motion in the water confirmed Ross's report that the steering was minimal.

In fact, in the clear silver light of early twilight, it looked worse than he'd said. As *Wind Shadow* closed in, Alix noted an entire row of broken, boarded-over portlights.

What she didn't see was the boat's captain.

Staring at the empty deck, she panicked for a moment. The boat looked derelict. Had Ross been swept overboard?

The distress she'd felt when he'd called her increased tremendously. Ross couldn't be dead. He simply couldn't.

Though the massive swells were making it difficult, she sailed her boat as close to *Sea Dreamer* as she dared. She shouted Ross's name. Over and over again she called as her ship slipped past his.

There was no answer.

Despite her intense desire to stop and check closer, the wind and the wave action were too strong. She was forced to sail on.

No response, she told herself. Not a sign of life on deck.

Dread began to build in her. As Alix sailed away, preparing to make another pass, she found herself remembering that moment when she'd decided not to call Ross Morgan. The moment when she'd laughed off the notion that if she didn't call, something drastic would happen.

Just as the goose bumps were beginning to well and truly crawl up her spine, she heard a shout.

She turned around and stared over her stern rail at the boat behind her. There was Ross, slowly climbing out of the cabin.

The wild wave of relief that hit her failed to temper the emotion that struck an instant later. How *dare* he put her through such distress?

The man should have been on deck waiting for her. Surely he had seen *Wind Shadow* approaching. A boat didn't just swoop down on someone unawares, after all. It took a while.

By the time she'd rounded up her boat and sailed it back to maneuver next to *Sea Dreamer*, Alix was very annoyed with Ross. She had intended for her first communication with him to be a courteous inquiry about his state of health. Instead, she shouted out, "What's the story, Morgan?"

Swaying with the motion of the swells rolling beneath his ship, he answered, "Rudder's smashed to smithereens. Mainsail's useless, boom's broken."

"Your portlights?"

"The plywood I covered them with is holding the sea at bay. Bad leaks, though."

His adjustments to his boat's motion seemed, she thought, to be awkward and stiff for such an experienced sailor. He looked weary. Lord, the truth was he looked half dead. She noticed a bandage wrapped around one leg.

"What's that?" she called across.

"Rudder shard got me."

"You went over the side in this storm?" Her disapproval was clear. *Are you nuts?* she was really asking.

"Had to."

"Sure."

She'd forgotten how blindly macho this man could be. Suddenly she was very, very sorry she'd decided to "just have one quick drink with the gang" on that fateful Tuesday evening in Fort Lauderdale. Without this asinine single-hander's race, she'd be happily riding out the storm with a crew member for company, well rested and well on her way to St. Thomas. Instead, she was preparing to deal with the *stupendous* headache that this rescue mission was going to be.

"How's your motor?"

He turned his thumb down.

"So, tell me, Ross," she shouted with fine cynicism, "what's the *good* news?"

He looked across to her. She could see the thoughts crossing his face. At one moment his lips started to move in what was obviously going to be a sarcastic retort. Then a final, inexplicable expression flickered across his exhausted features.

"The good news," he answered, "is that you're here."

Fifteen minutes later, Alix was beginning to feel as exhausted as Ross looked.

The fight to keep *Wind Shadow* lined up with *Sea Dreamer* in the heavy swells—without smashing into the other boat—was a tough one. It had degenerated into a yelling match as both their fatigue-frayed tempers unraveled even further. And now that the two boats were finally lined up, a position she couldn't hold for long, Ross was suddenly behaving in his typical, mule-headed fashion.

"I am *not* taking hold of that line, Alexandra."

She stared at the thick coil of rope that lay at

his feet; the other end of it was already well secured around both her cockpit winches.

"You have to, Ross. How the hell else are we
going to get the tow line hooked up? Am I supposed to pull *Sea Dreamer* along behind me by
the sheer power of ESP?"

"Sounds fine to me, sea witch. 'Cause there's
no way you're going to mesmerize me into pick-
ing up that line."

He was staring across at her, his arms so
tightly wrapped they looked locked together for
eternity.

"Damn it, Ross, I'm in no mood for games."

"Games? *Games?* Don't feed me that bull. You
know admiralty law as well as I do. I'll let *Sea
Dreamer* sink to the bottom before I'll hand you
salvage rights to her."

"Are you insane? Did this storm knock what
little brains you have loose? I don't want what's
left of your boat"—she surveyed the damages—
"I am *rescuing* you, fool."

"And if I accept that line from you, you own
Sea Dreamer. Legally. And *I'm* not about to trust
the word of someone who fakes her sailing re-
ports. You claim you don't want my ship now.
Tomorrow could be another story."

Her eyes raised to the rapidly darkening sky.

"Give me strength."

She didn't have time for this. The light was
fading. The swells were knocking the two boats
together; the bolsterlike plastic fenders that pro-

102

tected the hulls from impact were taking an awful beating.

It was clear this boat needed to be taken in tow, and it was equally clear that Ross was prepared to drag this ridiculous argument out for hours. Action had to be taken.

Fifteen seconds later, as the two vessels were thrown together, Alix implemented her decision. Lightly she leapt from *Wind Shadow* to *Sea Dreamer*. Grabbing up the heavy rope in one fell swoop, she hauled it to the mast and half-hitched the thick rope securely around it.

"There. That satisfies the letter of the law. Be it noted that you have not relinquished your ship, Captain Morgan." She glared at him. "Satisfied?"

She got no answer, at least not a verbal one. In dead silence he began assisting her in securing *Sea Dreamer* to be towed.

When the task was finished he still had not spoken a word. Alix, too, had kept her own counsel as she worked. She was uncomfortable with the situation and wanted nothing more than to return to her ship without speaking. But there were things that needed to be said.

She waited as he coiled a line, though it was obvious to her that his action was merely a way to avoid contact. When he finally laid it down she spoke.

"Ross, it's clear this race to St. Thomas is finished."

"Obviously." His words came hard and sharp. "You've won."

The very curtness of his words told her what losing meant to him. She saw his anger—a self-directed anger. She expected him to stay angry. But a number of subtle expressions, too complex to read, crossed the weary face. By the last, he seemed to have gained control of himself. When he spoke again his voice was almost courtly as he conceded to her, and she saw that he was sincere.

"I acknowledge your victory, Captain Boudreaux. The better pilot won."

A part of her wanted to accept his defeat—but only a small part. That competitive element of her personality was overshadowed by a growing sense of caring. Ross might be strong-willed to the point of pigheadedness, but he was a brave man too. She felt a rush of—no, it *couldn't* be love. . . .

Of course it wasn't. It was merely a natural human warmth, a perfectly platonic desire to offer someone who needed it some support, a sense of not being alone.

"No," she said to him gently, "the storm won. Neither one of us is winner or loser in this race. There *is* no race any longer. We'll forget this one, and run a new race in St. Thomas."

"Accept your victory, Alexandra. You deserve it. You are the better sailor. What I've done to *Sea Dreamer* proves that. I let my pride overrule reason. I failed my ship."

She couldn't deny that. It was true both knew it.

Looking at him, she saw how that tr upon him. His own conscience was I critic. Again she found herself impressed w... Ross. Strength in adversity, and responsibility. Two fine traits, traits that she valued highly.

"To admit what you just have takes courage, Ross. And I want you to know that I admire your strength, your integrity, in acknowledging it to me."

She moved a step closer. "Look. We have things to discuss before we head for landfall. Why don't we do it over a meal on *Wind Shadow*? I expect she's a bit dryer below decks than *Sea Dreamer* right now."

His softened attitude continued. "Take a quick look-see," he offered. "And view the just desserts of hubris."

She couldn't help laughing. But as she stepped down the companionway steps, her laughing stopped.

Alix wasn't shocked. She was too well aware of the damage even a single smashed portlight could wreak upon a cabin. But she was dismayed by the thought of Ross attempting to eat and sleep in the sodden mess that greeted her eyes. It was a disaster area. And from the looks of Ross, he was a walking disaster area himself. She was going to have to do something about that.

As she turned around on the step and glanced

ck at him, standing behind her in the cockpit, she knew that her "something" would have to be very carefully carried out. Though it appeared to be battered—not unlike his body—his pride was still an active factor here.

The sight of him—pride and pain juxtaposed—tugged at her heart. It brought back certain memories of her little brother, eleven years old to her sober, too-responsible seventeen. There was something in Ross's stance now that reminded her of Robbie when he would send her off to work with anxious assurances that he and Mom were going to be just fine, he knew how to take care of Mom real good, like the nurse had showed him, and the two of them were going to hold down the home front while Alix was gone.

"Alix. What's wrong?"

He was approaching her, full of concern.

"Nothing."

She shook her head, suddenly aware that her thoughts must have been reflected in her face. She tried to pass it off. "I think it was just seeing the coffee cup bobbing along like a purple duck down there—it blew my mind. That place is a first-class disaster area, isn't it?"

" 'Fraid so."

"Well, my place isn't. Let's get over there, let *Sea Dreamer* trail behind, and take a breather. I'd say we could both use it."

"No argument there."

When Ross set down his coffee cup an hour

later, he looked almost mellow. That was if you discounted the fatigue lines etched into his face, Alix thought to herself.

"Now that we've redefined the race," she started, "I think we—"

"Now that you've *won* the race," he corrected. "As far as I'm concerned, the race is over and you're the official winner. And I intend to inform Tully of the fact the next time you transmit to him."

She sent him a look of mock exasperation. "One-track mind."

"You bet."

"Well, track this. I want another race so I can prove fair and square that I can beat you. With both of us in fully operational boats for the entire course. *Without* northers, or other phenomena muddying the waters."

She leaned back into the bright yellow cushion behind her. "To me that means a day race, after *Sea Dreamer* is repaired."

"I won't get far arguing the point, will I?"

"No."

"All right. Another race when *Sea Dreamer* is fit."

Alix smiled. Ross looked secretly pleased. It was so nice to see another face on the ship after days and days alone. It was nice to see *this* face.

"What plans do you have for the prize money if you win the League Regatta?" he asked as he, too, settled into the comfortable cushions.

"The proof of my sailing ability will be the prize. Those men won't be able to argue that trophy away."

"Those men? Other captains, you mean."

She nodded.

"They've given you a lot of hassle?"

"Some. Women have just as much sailing ability as men do. And I think maybe healthier egos, because a number of the guys in the Charter Boat League have been expending a lot of energy trying to pump up their image by tearing down mine."

She brushed her hair back with a confident gesture. "This regatta will—if you'll pardon the expression—take the wind out of their sails."

Ross chuckled.

"So tell me," she continued, "what did you have planned for that prize money?"

"When *I* win?" He sent back that familiar brash grin of his. "What else? My heart's desire. My own charter service. Captain of my own destiny—if *you'll* pardon the expression."

The cheerful look faded. "That is, it's what I was going to do before *Sea Dreamer* was damaged. She was going to be the pride of my tiny fleet."

"She still will be," Alix reassured him. "We agreed on the Turks and the Caicos for a landfall, and we're about thirty hours away from the islands. They have a good boatyard. *Sea Dreamer* will soon be back to her old self."

108

"You sound as though you like my ship." He leaned his elbows on the table, and rested his head in his hands, looking at her.

"I do." She let her eyes roam over the lines of his well-muscled arms.

"Antiquated as she is, with that stayed rig of hers?" He tilted closer to her.

"There's a place for the traditional." She grinned. "It isn't first in a race, but there's a place."

"Hey, you." His voice was indulgent as he chastized her. "We've yet to prove that point, remember?"

"Oh yeah." She pulled one knee up, looking supremely confident. "I keep forgetting."

He glanced down at his empty cup. "Think there's a chance of a refill?"

"Nope."

She couldn't resist chuckling at his expression. "Coffee you don't need. Sleep you do."

"Oh, are we turning in?" His simple words dripped with sensual innuendo.

"*I* am taking the next watch," she said, then directed her coffee cup at him, "and *you* are turning in."

"This is one argument you won't lose, Alix." He stood up. "I am wiped out." He headed toward the companionway.

"The shower is that way," she called out pointedly.

"*Sea Dreamer* is this way." He put a foot on the bottom step.

"Ross." She waited until he was looking at her. "I don't want to have to pull rank. But you are on my vessel. And while you are, I am responsible for your welfare. Even a child could see that you need a good hot shower and some solid sleep in a dry bunk."

She saw the thunderclouds start gathering.

"If the positions were reversed, I have no question in my mind what you would do," she pointed out. "Tomorrow, when we start our voyage proper to the Turks, you'll be steering *Sea Dreamer*. If you're exhausted, you'll endanger us both. True?"

He sighed, and stepped away from the stairs. "Where's the shower?"

When Alix handed him some towels she also gave him a pair of sweatpants. "Here," she said, putting the soft navy garment in his hands, "this ought to fit you. What you've got on is so full of salt water it'll never dry."

"Would it do me any good to argue?"

"Not a bit. My berths are dry, and they're going to stay that way. I'm not letting any salt get into them." Once the salt settled in the bedding, she knew, it drew moisture and held it. The beds would stay clammy for the rest of the voyage.

She turned to go, brushing against him in the narrow confines. Such contact was inevitable in a boat, something she was well used to. That was why it surprised her to feel a sudden sensual flutter in the pit of her stomach from the brief encounter.

"Alix?" His voice stopped her. He looked down, and lifted his hand to brush the side of his thumb across her cheek.

Again she experienced that wild flash of desire. She found that her eyes couldn't leave his. The irises were the warm blue of a summer Caribbean sea.

"Thanks," he whispered.

She nodded, not willing to speak for a moment. Then she moved on. "Use the aft berth," she called behind her. "It's a double, big enough for you. And the motion is easy there."

"I will," she heard him say. "When's my watch?"

"In four hours," she answered as she started up the companionway. "Don't worry. I'll wake you."

She stepped off the top riser only to find him right behind her.

"You be sure that you do, Alix. You've been pushing pretty hard yourself."

"Yes." She felt disconcerted, looking down at him as he stood on the steps. A wild urge to kiss him welled up in her. Her lips suddenly ached for the touch of his, and her mind rebelled against good sense as well, flooding her with memories of their kisses before.

For a second she almost swayed toward him. Then she caught herself. Ridiculous. Ridiculous.

"Get that shower, and some sleep." She took a step back. "That's an order, Morgan."

Once more he spoke to her in the soft, sensual voice that did her in. "Aye, aye, Captain."

He disappeared down the steps. Alix took the wheel with her emotions in total disarray. What the hell was going on here?

What's going on here, she answered herself, *is that you've been alone for a long time, and now you're in the company—the solitary, closely confined company—of a man who from the start attracted you sexually.*

Once she'd defined the situation, she felt a little calmer. She checked behind her and saw that *Sea Dreamer* was trailing nicely, following *Wind Shadow* like a well-trained dog on an extremely long leash. Her mind at ease about Ross's boat, Alix set *Wind Shadow* on a course to the Turks and Caicos. For a while she steered standing up. Then the effects of her cup of coffee began to abate, and she decided to sit.

She rested her hand on the wheel and propped her foot against the base of the helm, putting herself in a favorite position. It was one that had always proved conducive to clear thought and the finding of solutions to knotty problems, such as the state of the economy and what to rustle up for dinner.

So, she asked herself, *what are you going to do about this?*

The answer wasn't simple. The possible resolutions ranged from tossing the man off *Wind Shadow* and ordering him to stay on *Sea Dreamer* the entire voyage to the opposite end of the spectrum—hopping straight into bed with him.

It seemed the middle of the road would be the most feasible. Friendly, but not romantic. Yes, she decided, that would be the ticket. Reserved would never work in such close quarters. Friendly it would be. Friendly, but fast on her feet.

Near the end of her watch three and a half hours later, she still felt a sense of satisfaction with the plan she had devised. Quietly, her boat shoes making no sound as she moved, she checked on Ross. He was solidly asleep in her berth.

On impulse, she checked her small alarm clock. It was set to go off in ten minutes; Ross was serious about taking his turn at the helm.

Oh no you don't, Captain Morgan. She punched the little knob. *You need sleep more than I do. And you're going to get at least two more hours of it.*

When she stepped into her cabin again she saw that he had hardly moved. His head was still nearly buried in her pillow, a lighter shadow in a cabin full of shadows. The dawn to come was only a glimmer of paler black in the eastern sky, a patch of charcoal through the portlight.

Sorry, Ross, she thought. She hated to wake him even now. But she was too weary herself. She could barely keep her eyes focused.

She lifted a hand to shake his shoulder. It hovered in midair, inches away from the bare, bronzed skin. She could feel the heat of his body radiating into her palm. The sensation caused a strange tingling in her fingers.

For over a minute she stayed motionless, absorbing the feelings, watching the shadowed face, her eyes tracing the strong, sharp planes. Each passing second increased her desire for him.

She felt emotion well up in her, so strongly it started a similar welling in her eyes, soft tears of tender feeling.

She wanted to caress his cheek, to whisper words of love. She looked at him another minute, filled with such thoughts. Then she sighed.

Remember, she told herself at last, remember the mistake it would be. She closed her eyes. When she opened them, she reached out and shook his shoulder lightly.

"Ross," she called quietly. "Ross. Time to wake up."

He slept on. She leaned closer, her mouth near his ear. "Ross. Come on now. Wake up."

He rolled slightly, and his head turned as he groaned. His eyes opened. They were staring at each other. His shift of position had them eye to eye, his mouth directly beneath hers.

As naturally as though it had happened a thousand times before, his lips gently caught hers, his arms reached up and he buried his fingers in her hair, pulling her head down.

In the gray, timeless predawn, it did seem perfectly natural. A dreaming reality. Alix joined her lips to his. Soft and slick, their mouths met in a slow erotic dance of desire.

And when his arms slid down to her shoulders and pulled her onto the bed, she joined him willingly.

CHAPTER EIGHT

Questions of yes and no, right and not right, all faded away. It was no longer important. Nothing was important but the way their bodies fitted together.

Alix was in another world. She let herself savor it, revel in it. Ross's arms were tight around her, holding her on top of him. His mouth was busily drawing wild shivers from her as it worked its way down her neck. The length of him felt hard and strong and very, very right.

Her own mouth was engaged in an assault upon his earlobe, nibbling away while her tongue flicked the soft flesh. She delighted in the slight moan that it evoked from him. When she traced the outline of his inner ear delicately with the tip of her pointed tongue, and felt him arch under her with pleasure, it sent her blood pressure soaring.

His hands had worked their way beneath the loose cotton folds of her shirt. Though the fingers and palms were storm-roughened, the sensation of his flesh upon hers was so erotic that she found herself aching for more.

Even before she could act upon her desire Ross was already pushing aside the neckline of her shirt to reach her breast, and as he kissed the soft white curve he, too, seemed unsatisfied with the fabric barrier, for his hand was slipping the buttons out of their buttonholes one by one.

Though one of her hands refused to leave the delights of his strong, warm shoulder, the other assisted him. Soon they were wrapped together, facing one another horizontally. His palms gently traced her curves as she engaged in similar exploration.

She found herself murmuring his name over and over. Her fingers trailed down his back, and dipped beneath the waistband of the sweatpants. Her teeth nibbled the yielding flesh along his shoulder. Her breasts pressed tightly against his chest. His hands slid the full length of her back, pulling her closer.

She was drowning in the feel of him, the scent of him, the taste of him. She wanted him, needed him.

As his mouth began blazing a maddeningly skillful trail toward her waist, the desire within started to overwhelm her. She arched to him as his lips and tongue tormented one rosy nipple, suckling, nipping, teasing. Each second built the frenzy that grew deep in the core of her being.

Yet the key to her undoing was the gentleness

117

of his touch. It was so unexpected from this powerful, forceful man that it was all the more erotic. She was melting within his embrace, spinning away into a hazy world of soft, sensual harmony.

In the ruddy glow of dawn's earliest light she could see his face. He was not the man she'd known. The hard planes seemed altered, softened. And his eyes . . .

She was losing herself in the warm intensity of their lapis-lazuli gaze. They looked into her soul with a gentleness and caring that seemed to promise the haven she had dreamed of for so long. Always the deepest part of her had ached for that unattainable prize—the serenity of love and security that life had thus far failed to provide. No conscious part of her mind even believed that it existed. It was only deep within that a hidden part of herself had continued to dream of finding such happiness.

Now here it seemed to be in the tender gaze of the man who held her.

Give in. Give in to it, Alix told herself. Take this joy.

Yet something within her would not surrender.

Was that only passion in his eyes—passion and nothing more, she wondered. Could she really believe that it was anything else?

All this she thought as he kissed her. And when she had absorbed that latest mental caution, when she could visualize beyond the moment and guess the future, she withdrew. Her lips dropped away and her head turned so those spell-binding eyes could not tempt her nor steal her private thoughts.

She felt him respond. His hold on her relaxed, yet his body took on a tenseness.

"Alix?"

It was a whisper as ephemeral as the dawning light. What she heard in its tone was a knife into her heart. It seemed to resonate with caring and concern. It made her want to hope for that which she dared not hope for.

She could not speak. Her throat was paralyzed with the bittersweet longing. She shook her head, refusing the question implicit in that one word he'd spoken.

His reaction was also wordless. She felt his hold upon her tighten in a convulsive, controlling motion. It was denial. Refusal to accept her with-drawal, both statement and demand.

"Alix. Come back to me." Again his arms pressed harder. "I want the woman I saw just now. Please don't run away."

One arm held her firmly. The other raised as his hand gently, so very, very gently, captured her chin and brought her around to face him.

"I know she's frightened," his voice soothed, "but it's safe here. It's safe here with me."

For how long? she wondered. For an hour? A night or two? Just long enough for her to get used to it, and then the warmth would desert her. Once again there would come the gaping emptiness, that black hole trying to suck her in, the same one she felt when her father had abandoned her.

The pain of that time became fresh. To her horror, it brought a sting of salty wetness to her eyes.

At that precise moment, Ross's head dipped to gain a clear view of her face.

She couldn't let him see her weakness. It was vital to keep up her position of strength with him. Yet she could see no way to escape.

Except one.

To hide her face and shield her vulnerability from him by embracing him in passion once more.

Her movement was abrupt, but it achieved her goal. It concealed her expression, though it was at the cost of once again experiencing the sweet agony of being in his embrace.

Why, why had it turned out this way? For so long she had struggled with the physical aspects of the issue of making love with Ross. It had seemed to be the only consideration. Her mind had not been weighed down with the emotional baggage that was now assaulting her, had never anticipated that to be in his arms could be more than a physical delight.

Again Ross was caressing her, though she could sense a puzzlement in him. She knew he did not understand what had transpired. Yet he seemed to be granting her what she had silently asked for—to ignore it and move on.

She would go through the motions a bit longer, she told herself, while she searched for a graceful way to end this before it reached a point of no return.

She began to nibble a path along his shoulder, her face well hidden. Though she tried hard to believe her own words, she could not hide from herself that to touch him, to hold him in her arms and kiss him was much more than "going through the motions." What she really was doing was stealing a few precious minutes more of the soul-sustaining reassurance she so desperately needed.

How had her perspective on this become so suddenly inverted, just because he had given her a tender gaze in a moment of passion? Why did she all at once have the feeling that to go to bed with this man would cause her to fall in love with him?

She had always resisted love before. She was strong. She had always been able to conduct her affairs with a lightness that threatened neither party. What had made her stumble this time?

Her hands were caressing his warm back, sliding down over the soft knit of his pants to savor the hard curve of his thigh. Her arm trembled slightly, and it was as much from fatigue as from passion.

Maybe . . .

Maybe, she contemplated, it was the stress of the past few days. The exhaustion, the lack of sleep. Such stress tended to weaken emotional stability, to break down the rational thought processes.

Yes. Surely that was it.

A stiffness she hadn't known was in her dissolved. She was safe. This overwhelming emotional response to him was due only to the chemical changes occurring in a brain when the body was overstressed. The feeling that was welling within her—this crazy impression that she loved him—was only a product of exhaustion. Nothing more. In a day or two, when she was better rested, the feeling would be gone. A good night's sleep would exorcise it.

As if her moment of relaxation was a signal of a more fundamental yielding, Ross increased his hold and became more intense, more demanding. It was clear to her that a decision had to be made. To stop—or to follow through to the inevitable conclusion.

The palest glimmer of saffron light fell through the porthole in a long, thin streak across the blue coverlet. Another shaft glanced off Ross's silver hair, now in a rumpled disarray that Alix found most appealing. She raised a hand and slid her fingers through the tumbled strands as he laid a soft trail of fire across her midriff.

Though the intimate connection of lovemaking *seemed* to be a threat, she told herself, that threat wasn't real. Her emotions might be temporarily vulnerable, but they would regain their balance. Physically, sharing love with this man was sheer heaven. The past minutes had made that abundantly clear.

Knowing all this, it would be cowardly for her not to acknowledge her desire and act upon it. After all, she had no doubt she could handle the consequences.

She reached to either side of Ross's face and pulled him gently to her waiting lips. As she did he seemed to read her decision in her expression. A low, gutteral sound emanated from deep in his throat, and his hands tightened in an ardent grip upon her hips, pulling her lower body against his. His head hovered over hers and his lips were crushing hers in a kiss that soon became equally powerful on both sides.

Their passion surged to a white heat that swept all before it. They were consumed in their own desire, aware only of each other and their own wild, wanton sensations.

The moment when they joined was slowly savored. But then Ross began to rock in a rhythm whose goal seemed to be to lay total claim to her. The pace, the intensity heightened, and it carried her with it. Her body filled with a sweet ache, a pleasure so vibrant that it was almost unbearable.

She was crying out his name, lost in sensation, carried to further heights by the sound of his own impassioned words, her entire being caught in a

123

maelstrom of ecstasy that built until she was the universe and the universe was her.

Moments out of time she was suspended there before she slowly spiraled down. Awareness of the world gradually returned to her. She was at peace, and yet filled with a wondering confusion.

Ross held her close. His lips covered her face with a flurry of kisses as soft as snowflakes. Then, smiling down at her, he gently stroked her cheek.

"Ah, Alix," he said to her, "you drive a man beyond his limits."

"What do you mean?" she asked, dismayed at how love-softened and breathless her words sounded.

"When we were making love just now, suddenly it wasn't enough, feeling you in my arms. I wanted you to be totally mine. For those few minutes I was driven to possess you."

She brushed a strand of hair away from her eyes. "You sound like you're apologizing."

"I am. No one has the right to own another like that." He settled more comfortably on the bed, making sure to keep her snugged against him. "It was temporary insanity. Brought on by your absolutely delightful, wild self."

"Oh, was it?" Her voice was husky and sardonic.

"Yes. It. Was." He affirmed, tapping her between the breasts with each word. The final time, his finger remained, pressing lightly on her sternum. As he continued to speak he let it veer off in a whimsical exploration of surrounding terrain.

"From now on, I'll—"

"From now on?" she asked breathlessly.

"From now on," he reiterated firmly, "our lovemaking will be a little more evenly balanced."

"What makes you think there'll *be* any more lovemaking?"

His finger stopped meandering along the under curve of her breast. His hand took possession of the entire alabaster globe, and he tightened his grip.

"Come off it, Alix." His eyes were burning with a chill blue flame. "Only you and me on this boat, baby. Nobody else here to put on an act for. Nobody watching, imposing social restraints of one kind or another."

His hand moved, sliding the palm over her nipple. "And if anything is clear from what passed between us"—he caught the pink bud with his thumb and forefinger as his hand slipped to cup the rounded fullness it held—"it is that we are absolute dynamite together."

Cool and slick, his mouth closed over the nipple. It did not draw back until he had elicited a tiny moan from her. "You see. We belong together."

She wanted to negate her physical response with yet one more flippant remark. But the words just couldn't get past her throat. Instead, she turned her head to stare out the porthole.

The rising sun was slanting across an ocean much calmer than the one it had set upon the evening before. The winds had died considerably. Things were almost back to normal.

Yes. Almost back to normal out there. But inside her cabin, the complications were only beginning.

Added to the jumble of other emotions swirling around within her was fear. We belong together, he had said. Did he mean as a couple? Was he talking about love? She didn't dare allow him even to start thinking in those terms. She would have to direct him away from *that* train of thought immediately.

"How do you mean, 'belong together'?" she questioned without turning her head back to look at him. "You do just mean in bed, I hope."

His stillness transmitted through to her body. She felt the complete absence of speech, of movement, as though it were a voiceless shouting. The nonsound got "louder" with each passing second.

"Of course," he announced at last. "My life is too full right now for anything else."

"Mine too." Her own tenseness was released like a puppet whose strings had been cut. She did not dwell on whether her response had been one of relief or collapse.

"Sometimes it seems," she went on, "that I'm doing more sea-spanning than Jason and all his argonauts."

Alix found herself pleased with how lightly

126

she'd spoken her dance-away sonnet. Her voice in no way had matched the pain inside. A pain that was false, she reminded herself. Just a transitory betrayal of the mind by a too-tired body. She intended to keep that fact uppermost in her thoughts.

Still she had avoided looking directly into his face. And she had received the oddest impression that when he'd answered her Ross hadn't wanted to look straight at her, either.

The silence now bothered her. It would turn awkward if it stretched on much longer. He might begin to question the sincerity of her noncommittal attitude. She was trying to determine what action to take to solve the problem when the question became moot.

Ross had initiated action on his own. It was such a compelling gambit that it took her breath away—literally.

His mouth had captured hers and begun to plunder it with renewed desire. Simultaneously he had seized her wrist and set her hand intimately against him.

She thought of fighting his unspoken demand, of getting up and leaving. But she knew that she valued what had transpired between them earlier too much to compromise it with an awkward retreat now. Then, as his own hands sought the sleek curves of her hips, she realized that the desire driving his demand was no greater than the desire within herself.

She faced that understanding and accepted it. Accepted, too, what it meant.

The passion deep inside her she allowed to blossom forth. Like the rising sun now blazing beyond the portlight, it consumed everything in its ascending path, enveloping them both in that ancient, eternal fire of the soul.

CHAPTER NINE

The self-appointed champion of traditional sailing stared up at the free-standing mast to where the rigging ought to have been. Ross could have been cursing the unseamanlike curve that the pressure from the wind in the sails put into it, dourly muttering to the ocean around him about aberrations. But he wasn't. Though his eyes were on the carbon-fiber pole, his mind was on Alix.

He was deep in thought, for assessing this complex woman was not easy. She was like a huge, kaleidoscope jigsaw puzzle, and he doubted that he would ever discover all the pieces, much less where they belonged. But he knew that in time he could put enough of them together to get close.

One elusive piece in particular was bothering him. He sensed it was a key motivator in her life. If he could find out what it was, and where it fitted . . .

Alix, Alix, he sighed mentally. What is the source of the pain in you that you tried to mask from me before we made love?

Whatever it was, it was motivated by fear.

He'd seen the emotion, the vulnerability in her green eyes. The fear wasn't of losing her independence. He was sure of it. On that score, he believed he already knew her well, for to know her drive for autonomy was to know his own. Neither one of them was weak enough in that area to have any doubt.

No, his intuition told him the hurt he'd seen in her was triggered from some past event.

A need to know what had caused it blended in him with an urge to ease her pain, to wash it away and replace the weight of unhappiness with joy.

He heard a clinking noise from belowdecks just then, and he smiled. Alix was awake.

"You slept well, my love," he chuckled beneath his breath.

He had left her so carefully that morning, easing out of the berth barely an inch at a time, to guarantee she got the same chance for a long sleep that she had given him.

Another rattling sound beneath his feet told him she was in the galley.

He wanted to go to her there, but deliberately he tightened his hand, which had been resting casually on the wheel. He had a boat to steer—two boats. He turned to look at *Sea Dreamer*. She was trailing nicely behind, as well-behaved as she had been when he'd checked ten minutes before. *You're too busy,* he ordered himself, *to leave the*

*helm and go running down the companionway just
to see her.*

Force of will—and pride—kept him at the
helm until her tousled head emerged from below.
Nothing, though, could keep the anticipation
from racing through him for those agonizing
minutes. Each little noise from below had tanta-
lized and tempted.

"Coffee?" she asked, standing halfway out the
companionway with a mug in one hand.

The brilliant tropical sunlight glinted off the
tumble of short blond curls, washing them with
highlights of vermeil, like a Renaissance painting.
"Angel in paradise," he whispered to himself.

"What did you say? I didn't hear," she said,
climbing the rest of the way up. She stepped into
the cockpit.

He watched her. She was acting so casual it
hurt. He had a sneaking suspicion that she was
going to play the "light and breezy" role to the
hilt.

A sudden spurt of anger hit him, though he
kept it hidden. Their lovemaking had been special, and he wasn't going to let her get away with
pretending it was business as usual. Yet he could
hardly wrestle her to the cockpit floor and hold
her there until she cried "Uncle." No, this would
have to be handled with a sure, smooth touch.

"I said 'paradise.' Coffee"—he pointed to the
cup in her hand—"and all this." His hand swung

out to take in the panorama of Caribbean sea and, seemingly incidentally, her.

She moved to hand him the cup.

"We should make good time today," she said in a casual tone. "How's *Sea Dreamer* handling?"

"I've always said she was a thoroughbred. Just look at her."

With his coffee cup well secured in one hand, and Alix's attention distracted to the ship behind them, Ross snaked his other hand around her waist and, with a peremptory tug, pulled her down beside him before she knew it.

"Good morning," he said into her startled face, and promptly kissed her.

It was a warm, sensual kiss, but he didn't elicit much of a response.

Her lips pulled away just as he thought the two of them were getting started.

"It's past twelve," she said, as though absolutely nothing had occurred. "Did you get a good noon sighting? Those scattered clouds lurking up there strike me as good sun-blockers."

"Oh no you don't, Alexandra Boudreaux."

Ross's coffee cup landed with an emphatic thump on the deck of the cockpit, and somehow the gesture was a declaration of determination.

"You're not going to get away with acting like nothing's changed between us."

This time he grabbed her with both hands, enveloping her in a powerful embrace. He kissed her as though his lips were a branding iron that would seal possession of her.

He'd known she would fight it. Known she was strong—but not as strong as he.

Even the battle was exhilarating. She had shown this morning that her passion was as powerful as her determination and her drive. Now he learned the lesson all over again. And at the end, as he had known he would, he came out the victor. But his margin was slight.

She would have left his side, but his hand was clamped around her wrist, a vise of male domination.

"Damn you, Ross Morgan. Damn you."

"For what? For showing you the passion you're made of? Or for not letting you bury it again?"

His hold on her was unbreakable. He knew she couldn't get up, couldn't leave, and he was prepared for a tirade from her.

But it seemed she had an unforeseen option— silence.

How could he decipher her feelings if she refused to speak? He had to get her talking. Defeat was unthinkable in this situation. The prize—understanding Alexandra—was too great.

"We need to have a serious talk here," he said to her.

"No we don't." Her mouth shut again.

He looked at the tight line. Those lips weren't sealed, they were Super Glued shut.

Alix's gaze was fixed straight ahead upon the companionway hatch.

Every muscle in her body was tensed for the possibility of action as she analyzed the options for removing herself from Ross's ridiculous macho power ploy.

Unfortunately, all she could focus on was how angry it made her. Male ego! It wasn't enough, the passion she'd displayed this past dawn. No, he had to hear it from her lips now, to wring a confession of desire, an admission of surrender to his prowess as a lover. Lord!

How it made her burn. Even though she knew that what he wanted her to say aloud was nothing more than a voicing of the truth. She rebelled against acknowledging to him that the lovemaking they'd shared had been incredible.

To admit that was to lose a portion of control over her life. He was already preempting her autonomy by this unbearable grip he had on her wrist. She'd never let him take even one more single, solitary bit of power away from her. *Her,* a woman who had commanded men just as powerful as Ross on many a voyage—

The light dawned. And Alix felt like kicking herself, for it was a mark of how strongly this man and his lovemaking had shaken her that it had taken her so long to notice the obvious.

She was careful not to let her mental grin of victory reach her lips. She'd soon have Ross Morgan in his place. All this craziness would be under control once more, and that control would be squarely in her hands—where it belonged.

"You seem to be well read on admiralty law," she commented, her eyes still on the companionway, "if your little performance over taking my line in your hand yesterday is any indication."

His surprise at the sudden break in her silence was apparent in the slight change in his hold on her wrist.

"Can you see how it applies in this situation?" she continued, honey and cream dripping from each syllable.

She paused. It was the kind of pause that Ross did so well, all mysterious and pregnant, with the promise of retribution to come.

The pause stretched on.

"No?" she queried when he failed to answer. "Then allow me to educate you."

Her head turned at last, and she met his impassive gaze with one of authority.

"The action you have taken here"—her eyes flicked down to her imprisoned wrist and returned to pin him with a chilling look—"can be construed in a court of admiralty law as insubordination, if not mutiny."

His grip only tightened, while the expression on his face—already grim—seemed to turn to stone.

"I am captain of this ship, Ross Morgan. I am the sole authority here while at sea, and you know full well that anyone on board *Wind Shadow* is subject to my command."

Now her ice-green gaze impaled him with the seriousness of her intentions.

"If your hand is not off my wrist within the next five seconds, I'll have you hauled before the board to have your captain's license reconsidered!"

"Watch that steering!"

Alix gritted her teeth together, biting back the bitter retort aching to slip past. As a small scraping sound echoed off the keel of her boat, she winced. When the sound repeated a few seconds later, she felt a sickening, sinking sensation in the pit of her stomach. Her fingers cold and tight on the wheel, she inched it to the right.

The sound stopped.

Before she could release the pent-up breath of apprehension that she'd been holding, the voice two feet behind her began haranguing again.

"Listen here, baby. If *you* run aground in this damn channel, *Sea Dreamer*'s gonna ram right up your transom. She's gonna slice you in two and leave your precious *Wind Shadow* lying on the bottom, just one more hazard to trap decent sailors navigating this godforsaken channel."

Ah, the sweet, dulcet tones of a thwarted male, she thought. And they say that hell hath no fury like a *woman*.

Well, right behind her—one foot wedged on

the bow of his boat and the other braced against the transom of her craft, with himself the only force keeping the two from ramming together—was a man who had completed this run to the Turks and Caicos in the highest of dudgeons.

When she'd given Ross her ultimatum, it had taken him less than five seconds to release her. And not a great deal much more than that to get himself off her ship and back onto *Sea Dreamer*. The entire operation had been carried out in glacial silence on his part.

Alix stared down at the clear green waters. Somehow, she thought, the silence had been the hardest part to take.

She hadn't expected the pain.

She'd been so angry. Anger could pump you up, carry you through difficult situations. If he'd shouted at her, if she'd been on the receiving end of a wild scene, she would have thrown her anger right back and felt it was justified. But the pain implicit in his silence, the unspoken accusation that she had countered with heavy artillery where only tactical fire was required—multiplied by her guilt at knowing anger had led her to blackmail to achieve her "freedom"—left her feeling like the lowliest of bottom-hugging barnacles.

No, she hadn't expected the pain. It had been her constant—her only—companion for the rest of the short voyage. Ross's continuing bitterness, though, was slowly alleviating her guilt. He, too, was carrying his chagrin to an extreme.

Harassment was inappropriate. The channel into the harbor was a tricky one, demanding full concentration. There were coral reefs lining either side, and navigating the waterway was no seafaring picnic. It demanded a great deal to navigate this channel single-handed. She could really use a crew member positioned up on the bow to call out directions and warn of dangerous coral formations. But of course she had no one.

Alix heard a grunt behind her, followed by a muffled curse.

To be fair, she thought, Ross was having an even harder time of it. With coral everywhere, they had needed to put *Sea Dreamer* on an extremely short line. She really was chasing up *Wind Shadow*'s transom. He was stuck with using his body as a buffer to prevent a collision. *Sea Dreamer*'s inertia—and the solid wooden boat carried quite a mass—would literally smash and sink her boat if it hit.

The strain on Ross's body must be tremendous, she reminded herself as she eased the wheel carefully to the right to avoid a huge coral head. That in itself was bound to produce some fallout in the "terse remarks" department.

She ought to make allowances. After all, she felt pretty uptight herself. Her entire body was tensed from the constant threat of ramming into an outcropping of the razor-sharp coral. Her eyes burned from staring so hard into the sea, despite

Polaroid sunglasses that reduced the glare of the sun on the water.

Lord, it seemed like they'd been doing this forever. And they still had miles to go. Nerve-racking. It was all nerve-racking. Even the steady put-put of her engine as it slowly pushed the boat forward was grating on her nerves.

"Port, damn it, *port.*"

Ross was shouting again. "Keep the boat to the center, woman, or we'll be eating coral."

Alix made the minor adjustment to the wheel that was required to stay on course and sighed. It was only midmorning, but she was prepared to stand behind a prediction. It was going to be a long, long day.

Twelve hours later, she gained little satisfaction from the fact that she'd been dead on the money. The day had been rife with hassles. And it was not yet finished.

"Look, mon," the voice of Jack Mauly, manager of the boatyard, was saying to Ross in his distinctive, lilting Bahamian cadence, "the t'ing is this. The rudder is completely gone. Not'ing left but a nub. So there is not'ing there to make a mold from to build you one. It's wiser to order a new rudder and ship it here."

His shoulders beneath the soft knit of his "I Love New York" T-shirt shrugged. "We'll make you a new rudder, mon, if that's what you truly want. But we cannot guarantee it will work as well as the one designed for your boat. What is your rush, anyway?"

"I have to be in St. Thomas."

"But this lady is also going to St. Thomas. I heard her say so earlier today. What is the problem? You sail with her. You come back for your boat when the rudder gets here."

As the mulish look that had become all too familiar to Alix crossed Ross's face, the expression on Jack's altered to one of perplexity.

"There is no way you can carry that boat to St. Thomas. That would be crazy. You were lucky to get it here. Why are you so stubborn when you have a friend who can take you where you need to go?"

"Yes, Ross. Why so stubborn?" Her voice was filled with sarcasm. "Is your ego so fragile that you're incapable of crewing anymore?"

She had spent the day aching to get away from this man's company. But now she was not only insulted at his attitude toward traveling with her, she was hurt. If she could have found the time, and the peace, to analyze her feelings, she would have realized why. But Alix was a woman of action, at the end of a day filled with frustrations, and was suffering from an ailment she'd never experienced before. She would have been as surprised as anyone to discover that ailment was love.

So she had no idea why her common sense

short-circuited at that moment, freeing her to re-act as she did.

"You see," she confided in a stage whisper to Jack, "you are in the presence of a man who is such a great captain that to serve as a deckhand would be a fall from grace."

"Cut it, Alix."

She turned a stony look on him.

This man had made love to her, had almost, *almost,* exposed her vulnerability, had even been determined to make her admit that vulnerability. Now he was equally determined to walk away. He deserved to hurt like she was hurting.

"Why, Ross." Incredulous innocence fairly dripped from her voice. "I'm just telling it like it is."

"I said cut it."

His jaw, his fist, in fact every bit of him, was tensed with anger. The anger was at least fifty percent self-directed.

He'd known Alix wasn't a woman who could be pushed, he told himself, and still he had tried. He'd known stubbornness and pride led to cut-your-nose-off-to-spite-your-face situations, and still he had sailed directly into the gale.

Jack appeared to be following the dictum that the better part of valor was discretion. He was saying not a word. Indeed, he seemed not to know which one even to look at, for his focus kept shifting between the two. But Ross knew who to stare at.

Alix stood near him, proud, angry, beautiful. Each of those elements tugged at him. Yet most poignant of all was the carefully masked pain he sensed beneath the surface. He realized that he was aching for her in a dozen different ways, and only one of them was sexual.

Still, the tilt of her head as she met Jack's flickering gaze made Ross think of the way she had tilted her head when she looked at him as they lay together after making love. The memories of that night washed right over his anger and frustration. Unfortunately, they set up a whole new set of frustrations.

What the hell had he been doing? Pride was no substitute for holding Alix in his arms once more.

It was true that he had no wish to crew. He'd been born to command, and he knew himself well enough not to deny that fact. But he was also intelligent. And clearly the intelligent thing to do here conflicted with that pride.

There comes a time in a man's life, Ross told himself, when he must face the fact that events have brought him to a junction that could change his life forever. He saw now that he was at such a point.

The choice loomed before him. There was no time to ponder all the ramifications. It was keep his dignity and lose Alix—or humble himself. Immediately and fully.

He braced himself for the killing blow.

"Stubborn? Me stubborn? What makes you

think that, Mr. Mauly? I'd be more than happy to crew on Alix's boat in order to get myself to St. Thomas. But, you see"—now he was confiding in the manager—"it's not up to me. Captain Boudreaux may not want me on her ship. And a gentleman does not force the issue by asking to come where he's not wanted."

"Yes, Mr. Morgan, I see that."

Jack nodded his head at the logic of Ross's thinking. His dark brown eyes looked at Alix. There was the slightest tug at the corners of his mouth.

"Have I made an untrue assumption? This man is *not* welcome aboard your ship?"

Alix felt like shaking her fist at the unkind fates that were having a field day screwing up her life. She had wanted Ross to ask her for a berth on her ship. But she had wanted that request on the heels of an abject apology for venting his frustrated male ego for the past day and half. After his retreat to his own boat, and his surly attitude while she was towing *his* boat to port—using up her fuel to motor-sail them in, no less—the least she was owed was some genuine groveling from him.

Yet, was she going to get it? Oh, no. He had neatly maneuvered the situation in front of a witness so that *she* would look like a prime turkey if she made Ross squirm. In fact, she would look like a full-course Thanksgiving dinner if she

143

didn't paste on a smile and invite him on the passage to St. Thomas.

She glanced at Ross, who actually did not have the gloating expression on his face that she expected to see. Why was that?

Then she noticed the boatyard manager was still looking at her, waiting for an answer.

Was Ross welcome on her ship? Suddenly an image of her cabin, with the dawn light spilling over their naked bodies tangled in the coverlet of the berth, filled her head. Memories of their lovemaking tumbled through her mind, generating an unexpected ache deep within her.

It would happen again. Sailing for days, alone together in the cramped quarters of her small boat—oh yes, it would surely happen again. And she knew that would lead to caring for him, caring deeply.

Could she accept that? Could she handle it?

As she asked herself these questions, almost certain that the answer was no, her mind tossed in another from deep in left field. Maybe she wasn't emotionally prepared for it right this minute. Maybe she should have more time. But years from now, would she be able to live with the fact that she had allowed cowardice to rule her? She had never before experienced the emotions this man engendered in her. If she ran away from that, if she dodged the responsibility of facing up to the feelings she had for Ross, if she let pride be used as an excuse for what she knew deep down was really fear, could she live with the knowledge she had run from life instead of facing it head-on? She had never run before. Not even in the blackest moments. Difficult as her problems had been, she had moved forward and battled them. Even when her mother had been dying, she had held herself together and done what had to be done. If that had not defeated her, how could she let this?

Jack was still politely awaiting a reply, she noted belatedly, though he looked a little uncomfortable at the way the silence had stretched on. Clearly he thought the delay was because Ross truly was unwelcome on *Wind Shadow,* and Alix was reluctant to come right out and say so publicly.

Her gaze turned to Ross. He, too, must be thinking the same thing. It appeared not to affect him, beyond a sardonic little twist to his mouth.

But Alix knew the score between them. She had looked upon that face after they had shared the most intimate of physical encounters, and she could read faint signals that would be invisible to most people.

Case closed.

"No, Mr. Mauly," she answered at last, "your assumption was correct. A man of Ross Morgan's abilities is more than welcome upon my ship."

CHAPTER TEN

Hot. So hot.

Alix dropped her head, rubbing the back of her sweat-dampened neck. One bare foot listlessly draped over the bottom of the wheel. She nudged the curved metal tubing slightly to the right with her big toe.

Wind Shadow responded effortlessly to the course correction. Not that it made much difference, she thought dourly. With the wind moving at one or two knots, she wasn't going anywhere in a hurry.

She pulled her sticky shirt away from her midriff, trying to force some air under it. This was really a day for wearing a swimsuit. But with Ross on board that seemed too much of an invitation.

Her hand ran through her damp curls. The last two nights had, as journalists phrased it, "passed without incident."

Though she was thinking longingly of how what little breeze there was would slip over her in her two-piece, she reminded herself that the wisest course would be to do nothing that might provoke a change in that status.

Of course, she reflected as her foot eased the wheel an inch to the right, she'd been surprised that things were progressing so sedately. She really had expected Ross to begin a seduction campaign that first day out. He hadn't. She had mentally prepared herself for intimacy, but he was holding back. This is fine, she'd told herself, my problem is solved. No intimacy means no emotional entanglement. This is just what I wanted.

So she had quite naturally been dismayed to discover that the sight of this man's body was driving her crazy.

Awareness of his physical presence had become a constant, nagging ache.

"Alix?"

There he was, climbing out of the companionway. And, very sensibly, he was wearing nothing but a pair of swimming trunks. Silently she groaned. Every inch of him—from his silver-white hair to his toast-brown toes—was a bronzed god.

"I'd like to shoot a star or two, if you don't mind."

"Mind?"

She presented him a perfectly bland face. *I mind the way the muscles on your chest ripple as you pull yourself out of the companionway. I mind the way the twilight turns your hair to pure silver. I mind the way your lips lightly part and your*

tongue slides along them to lick off the salt spray.
I mind the way your suit delineates the taut planes
of your hips—

Her foot gave the wheel an unnecessary push. "No, I don't mind."

He flashed her a grin and made his way to the stern. One leg swung over, then he wedged the foot against the gunwale. With his body thus braced, he raised the sextant he carried in one hand.

Alix tried hard to look nonchalant as he steadied the instrument before his eye. When it came to shooting sun sights, she could hold her own. But she had never learned the more complex celestial navigation. Of course, sun sights were more than adequate for determining a course, but the mark of an expert navigator was his ability to steer by the stars.

Ross was lowering the sextant, and the action puzzled her, for the instrument had been held to his eye for less than ten seconds.

"Say," he said, "why don't you shoot too? If we compare fixes, we should get a reading that's right on the money."

Suddenly the heat wasn't bothering Alix. In fact, she felt downright cool. Her status as a sailor equal to Ross was about to be destroyed. He was going to find out she couldn't shoot stars.

He was smiling at her. A friendly smile, a reasonable smile.

Surprisingly, Ross had been—dare she call it

mellow?—since that evening at Jack's boatyard. He almost seemed like a man she could trust. To let the Ross Morgan she'd known before discover that she didn't know celestial navigation would have been like volunteering to walk into a buzz saw, with about the same probability of survival. He would have ripped her up, chuckling wickedly throughout. Yet as she looked at him now, she was tempted to be honest and just tell him that she didn't know how to shoot stars.

He was still looking at her, a smile on his face.

She could wiggle out of it. He need never know she didn't equal him in this area. Yet to do that would be to admit to herself that she didn't trust him, no matter how he behaved.

Was that true? With Ross waiting for her answer, she quickly examined the issue. She thought over all that had happened between them. When she'd done so she realized the only time dishonesty had come into play was when she'd misrepresented her true feelings for him. Then she remembered the way he had wanted to talk the afternoon following their lovemaking. She had been the one who shut him out.

It looks like I'm *the one who can't be trusted completely.* She moved her foot and locked the wheel into position. It was time to balance the ledger—to offer some honesty.

"I'd be happy to oblige you, Ross, but"—she set her hands on her knees and looked directly at him—"I don't know how to shoot stars."

Alix would have thought the surprise on his face was comical if she hadn't felt so vulnerable.

"To tell you the truth," she continued, "I never thought it was all that vital. Sun sights do the job."

His leg slowly swung back over the gunwale. He moved across the deck and joined her.

"It's true, they do. Star sights allow you to pinpoint more exactly, of course." He shifted the sextant in his hands, staring down at it.

"I've watched you take a sun sight, Alix. I'll vouch that you know how to calculate position."

She grinned at him wryly. "Thanks."

"I'd be happy to teach you, if you're interested."

She searched him for traces of condescension, but found none. Still, she hesitated. She wanted to learn how to take star sightings, but not at the cost of looking like a fool by possibly screwing up the lesson in front of him.

Perhaps Ross guessed that, for he sat back and started talking casually about the topic.

"With the new HO249 tables, celestial calculations are simple now, once you've figured out your general latitude and the Greenwich hour angle of area. It's just a matter of looking it up in the tables. You can forget all that garbage about declination, sidereal hours, T or Z angles. Today it's only a matter of subtraction."

"Really?" She let herself sound only vaguely interested.

"Really. What do you say? Are you up to the challenge?"

She closed her eyes for a brief second. Did the man know what button to push, or had his question just been accidental? How could she walk away from a challenge?

"Let me get my sextant and I'll be right with you," she answered.

"Don't bother. We'll use mine. It will be easier, it has a light for the arc."

"Sure," she agreed. And she knew she was agreeing to much more than that. She was agreeing to let him take the lead.

He looked to the twilight that was rapidly fading, then at his watch. It was on Greenwich time, she noted with admiration. Another mark of a good sailor, since Greenwich time was the basis for longitude calculations.

"We've got to move like lightning if we want to get our sights," he said, stepping back to the gunwale. "We probably don't have more than an eight-minute window left for catching both the horizon and the stars."

It was exactly what he called it, an "evening-star circus," as they rushed around trying to catch the various stars in the small sight and take their elevation within the narrow time frame.

"Lord, the stars are tiny. How can I keep this pinprick of light in there?" she complained, staring into the prism at the almost nonexistent point of light that was Polaris.

"That's the art of it," he replied. "Anyone can do the chart. The skill lies in resolving those double images."

"I see," she replied with a sardonic tone that made him chuckle. But she renewed her concentration and managed to capture the North Star.

"Four seconds equals a mile," she muttered to herself a little while later, staring intently at the second hand sweeping around her watch. If she was off by two seconds, she'd have their position off by half a mile.

In five minutes she had shot six stars, running all over the boat to do so.

As Ross watched her capture star after elusive star in the sights of his sextant, he had to admit he was impressed. Alix was one sharp lady. In no time she'd picked up the tricky handling required.

One sharp lady, and one sexy lady. Yes, a very special lady indeed. Worth the sizable piece of crow he'd had to eat in order to end up on her boat. Well, he thought, as his captain finished her latest sighting, a person had to give in order to get. And what he was going to get would be more than adequate compensation. It had been a mistake to try to force an admission of caring from her. But this time, with a different approach— with time and consideration—he would gain access to those inner thoughts she hid so well.

Look at the sparkle in her eye right this minute, he thought with pleasure. She'd been dashing around the boat mastering star sights. He smiled, moving toward her as she turned and began rushing across the cockpit to catch her last star before the horizon faded.

At that moment a freak puff of wind hit the sails. The boat rocked at the sudden gust, and Alix pitched forward as her foot tangled in a coiled line.

Ross lunged toward her, catching both her and his sextant at the last second.

Adrenaline pumped through his system, making his body quiver slightly as he absorbed the impact of her fall and landed on the deck. His body cushioned her fall, his arms protected her— and the sextant.

A sharp retort was on the tip of his tongue; a sailor's sextant was sacred, and for her to drop it would have ruined the expensive instrument. But then he thought of Alix being injured by the fall, and his irritation melted.

"Careful, my friend," he cautioned in a low voice.

His arms curved tighter around her. She was sprawled across him, her arms captured within the circle of his. Her body felt so right, so unbelievably soft and right on top of him.

"Ross." Her voice was a ghost of sound. "I'm so sorry." Her hand still awkwardly gripped the sextant. It was digging into his ribs.

"Here." Without releasing his embrace, he used one hand to remove the sextant from her and set it down carefully. Then he shifted until his back was against the bulkhead of the cabin. "Now then. No damage done. The sextant's fine."

Perhaps the sextant is. But I'm not.

Alix allowed herself to remain in Ross's arms. *I'm just catching my breath,* she thought. But she knew she didn't want the moment to end.

She had missed the feel of his embrace. She had known that. But she hadn't realized until this minute how very much she had missed it. She was breathing in that special scent that was Ross, drinking in the press of his flesh against her. His lips were only inches from hers, and she felt the warm fanning of his breath, a soft zephyr that set her mouth to tingling.

In the next instant she saw the expression on his face alter, and she knew from the way each hard line turned gentle, the way his lips softened and his eyes turned a melting blue, that he was going to kiss her.

Her mouth reached out to his at the same moment, and they joined in the most ephemeral of touches. Slowly, slowly, infinitely slowly they increased the pressure, tasting, exploring with each and every subtle advance.

She and Ross surrendered into an embrace that was timeless. Their lips seeking, playing, advancing, retreating, engaging. Their arms holding, touching, caressing, molding, fusing. Their bodies pressing, sliding, yielding, demanding, dissolving . . .

He was holding her, and she was floating in the warm Caribbean breeze that caressed her limbs, he was lifting her up in the air, and her head was spinning, whirling. He was looking down at her, and those fathomless, loving eyes were asking the question his voice would not, or dared not, ask.

She felt like she was spinning away into a strange and unknown world. Ross was pilot on the journey, and now he was asking if she wanted to join him in full exploration or pull back to the sanctuary of her solitude.

She knew the risks; she understood the dangers. Yet their importance faded before the depth of feeling that was flooding her as she looked into his face. Her answer to the eloquent plea in the cobalt eyes was to return his gaze and let him see her own desire and caring reflected back.

She followed with a tightening of her embrace, her head pressing into the firm wall of his chest. With a swift, grateful motion, his arms increased their pressure. He swung her over one of the thin foam mats that cushioned the long molded seats in the cockpit. As he settled her reverently upon the red canvas that covered the mat, she reached her arms up to him. A moment he stayed above her, one finger catching a tendril of gold and carefully brushing it back into the tumble of silken loops that spilled onto the scarlet cushion.

Then he spread his long, hard body over her like a shield.

The sensation was one of being protected and desired and cherished simultaneously. She wanted it to go on forever. Her arms held him, closer, closer, willing it to go on forever. Above her the stars burned, a thousand blue-white diamonds scattered over a dark violet-blue banner. The sea was a gentle, murmuring chorus; the breeze, soft curling caresses that lay with a cool hand over those parts of her that Ross's heated form did not cover.

Their voices joined the deep sounds of the ocean. Mewling little cries of desire, gentle whispering pleas, ardent urgent sighs. The slow rocking of the boat left them with each other as the only stability in their universe. They joined together, fusing their separate passions into one blazing critical mass.

The sky, the ocean, everything around them faded as they explored a plane where the imperatives of time held no dominion, wrapping them in an ever-expanding, all-consuming firestorm of passion. As the power of it overcame them, they were swept into a nova of exploding desire that burned until nothing remained but the essence of their intertwined souls.

Some small eternity later, Alix became aware of the gentle lapping of the waves against the hull of *Wind Shadow*. Ross lay quietly beside her, his head resting against her shoulder, one hand spread with gentle possession across her stomach.

At first she felt only peace and contentment. Then gradually a sensation built within that eroded her serenity.

Physically she still felt marvelous, but emotionally she felt as if she were teetering on a precipice. There was no reason for it, no reason in the world, yet she was on the verge of tears.

Ross's lips were upon her shoulder now with slow, soft butterfly kisses. His head raised, and he smiled into her eyes.

"Happy?"

Unable to answer his question, she buried her head into his surprisingly soft hair, hoping he would take the gesture for an affirmative.

It seemed he was more perceptive than that, though.

"Alix." His hand was stroking her hair. "Something, some pain, is stirred up when we become intimate. I want to help with that." He drew her close in a protective embrace. "Tell me about it. Let me help you ease the hurt."

"Ross, please." Her head moved in denial. "You're imagining," she said, even as the pain within grew stronger.

"Alix, Alix. We both know better." The tenderness in his voice tore at her heart. This caring felt so real. How was she going to bear it when it disappeared, just as her father's love had evaporated?

"I don't talk about it."

"You do with me." Though the loving tone remained, his voice was firm. It accepted no evasion. "With me you don't need to hide your weaknesses. I am here for you, love. I won't let you carry this sadness alone."

His head shifted, moving away so he could look into her face. "Burying it won't make it go away, you know."

Each word he spoke made her foolish need to cry grow stronger. If she broke down, how could she go on? How could she be Captain Alexandra Boudreaux, master of *Wind Shadow,* after he had seen her cry?

"No, Ross," she insisted, tight-throated with her effort to hold in the tears.

"Yes, Alexandra," he countered lovingly. His voice was little more than a whisper. "Yes, my beautiful, sad captain. You're going to tell the man who loves you. And together we're going to fix it."

It was too much. His words of love demolished her defenses. She tried to speak, to begin the explanation of her secret pain. But on the first syllable she burst into tears.

In the safety of his arms, she allowed her hurt to break free of the barriers that had held it in. Great racking sobs shook her; years of repressed pain were dredged up and expiated in the salt of her tears.

For a long time she only cried as he held her

close, and she could feel him trying to transmit through his body the comfort he so desperately wanted to give her. Then slowly, through her broken sobs, she began to explain to him.

"So you've always felt abandoned," he said a few minutes later as he began to comprehend her disjointed narrative. "Always felt it was your place to hold things together, to carry the burden of responsibility."

Again his arms held her tight. "Oh my sweet girl, how hard life has been for you."

His words were like a balm on her heart, for she felt the sincere caring behind them. It was not pity he offered, but empathy.

"It was so abrupt," she explained, able at last to speak without breaking into sobs. "So complete. He just walked out one day, and never even called again. We were on our own, my mother and two children. I was thirteen, my brother just a kid."

"And you started taking on responsibility."

"Cooking and cleaning at first. Mom took to working two jobs to make ends meet. I added baby-sitting money. Then I got a part-time job."

"And another and another." He kept her carefully snugged into the haven of his body. "You must have begun to see male love as a basically unreliable gift that leaves you with nothing but trouble and pain. Isn't that right?"

"Does it show that much?"

"Let's just say that knowing what I know now,

it makes a logical explanation for your attitudes and behavior since we met."

She sighed, settling closer to the comforting warmth of him. Her hands rested lightly on his chest. The slow rise and fall of his chest was a rhythm that filled her with a sense of security.

"You've had more pain than most, Alix. And you've survived it. But it seems to have cost you something very precious—the love between a man and a woman."

His lips moved close to her ear. One of his hands raised and a finger gently brushed her cheek. "You've been afraid to take that risk. But now it's time to trust. It's time to love again, Alix." His voice was just a gentle breath fanning her ear. "Love me, Alix. Love *me.*"

She felt herself sinking again, wavering on the edge of that precipice. Where was the guardian with its sword of righteous protection? Where now, when she needed to retreat and rearm?

"And who are you, Ross Morgan? I don't know you." Her hands slid away from his chest. "You are one man here, and another entirely when racing *Sea Dreamer* or holding your own at the drinking table. How can I believe this man is real?"

"Don't you recognize trust when it's given?"

Surprised, she looked at him, though she'd been doing her best to avoid his eyes. She read the truth there. This was a Ross Morgan only she would see. This was a man who loved her.

In that moment of truth, she banished the guardian who had isolated her heart. For there was only room now for the love she knew she felt for Ross, a love that had grown within her, unnamed and unrecognized, until he illuminated the shadowed corners where it had come to life.

Her gaze softened. Her arms returned to slide around him. Her lips dipped to place a soft kiss upon the center of his chest. Then she spoke, her voice a whisper, throbbing with an emotion long repressed.

"Don't you recognize love when you see it?"

CHAPTER ELEVEN

"Hey, hey, *hey!*"

Lifting her hand from the chart where she'd just finished plotting the last twenty-four hours of progress, Alix chuckled. Ross must finally have hooked a fish.

As she stowed her instruments, she smiled a private, indulgent smile. Her man had been at it for half the morning. So far he'd caught some excellent specimens of seaweed, but seaweed had never been a particular luncheon favorite of hers.

With a practiced twist of the wrists, she rolled up the chart. She'd begun to think she was going to have to open a can of tuna if they were going to have seafood for lunch.

Please don't let this one slip off the hook, she pleaded with an amused sniff, *like his last two "sure" catches.*

Just as she stowed the featherlight tube, she heard another shout.

"Baby! Hey, baby! Get up here and take a look at the most beautiful bit of lunch you ever saw!"

Alix bounded up the companionway steps,

ready to share his enthusiasm. The truth was, she hadn't been out of good spirits since the night they'd made love under the stars. They had not slept that night, not until it was nearly dawn. For hour upon hour they had shared their inner thoughts, their fears and hopes, their dreams. In short, they had shared loving. It was only late the next afternoon that Alix realized they had made love three times throughout that long, languorous night.

Now she laughed as she stood at the top of the steps, watching him flaunt a large rainbow-bright fish, its yellow tail flashing in the sun. *Mahi-mahi* the Hawaiians called it. In the Caribbean it was known as dolphin. Of course, it was nothing like the true dolphin. No, this was a delicacy, a true fisherman's delight. Lunch was going to be a gourmet affair, after all.

The fish was twisting wildly on the line, its tail flapping as its body arced.

"Hey, toss me a winch handle," he called.

She knew he intended a quick blow to the head to finish it off. She answered with a negative shake of her head and disappeared down the companionway.

"Alix. Come on," he shouted. "Don't start playing tricks on me now."

She reappeared. In one hand was a bottle of rum. The other was gripping the handle of a yellow plastic bucket.

"Let's take care of the fish first, and *then*

party," he said, a slight tone of exasperation creeping into his voice. "All right?"

"Forget the winch handle," she replied, a saucy smile curving up the corners of her mouth. "We're going to show a little elegance here."

Moving to the stern of the boat, she dipped the bucket and drew it back up, partly filled with seawater.

"What are you doing, woman?"

"You'll see."

The bucket landed on the deck with a little sloshing sound. The clink of the rum bottle followed as she set it down and trapped it in place with one foot. Her body straightened. She opened her palm. "Hand over the fish, please."

Ross threw her a skeptical, if not annoyed, look.

"The fish, Ross," she repeated.

With a shrug, he relinquished it. Taking the fish by the tail, she held it upside down in the bucket, its snout in the salt water. The fish slowed its mad struggles.

Gently she opened one of the gills, then picked up the rum bottle and poured in a dollop of rum. She repeated the process on the other gill. The fish went limp.

"There you are, Captain Morgan. One dolphin, peacefully sent to his reward, and ready to be cleaned."

"You, woman," he answered, grabbing her around the waist, "are full of surprises."

"Oh yeah?" she laughed back, trying to land a kiss on his mouth. The motion of the boat sent her balance off, and the kiss landed half on his ear, half on his jaw.

"Yeah." He shook her with mock anger, then laughed himself. "And you certainly have a knack with fish, even if your kissing radar is two sheets to the wind."

"Well, we'll see what kind of a knack *you* have when you dish up our lunch."

"Hey, I've been fishing all morning."

"Yes, indeed. And I've been steering. *And,* since it's still my watch, *you* are the designated galley slave."

She stepped back from him and set hand on the wheel, grinning victoriously.

"Ah well." He lifted the fish. Holding it up high, he looked the deceased yellowtail in one glassy eye. "What can you expect? These Captain Bligh types always try and throw their weight around. What there is of it."

Ross moved off to the cabin. "Tell you the truth," he confided to his defunct companion, "I really enjoy it when she starts tossing that weight. For instance, the other night she threw herself on me just when I . . ."

His voice faded as he disappeared from view.

Alix was torn between laughing and pitching the rum bottle down after him. She settled for a silent chuckle.

When he appeared with lunch she decided the

soundless chortle had been the wisest course. After all, if she'd conked him with the bottle, or miffed him with her laughter, she might have done herself out of the fabulous feast he was setting before her.

Broiled mahi-mahi with fresh lime, fried plantain courtesy of the stalk they had laid in at the Turks, rice sautéed in butter with onions, raisins, and almonds—it all looked delicious. Two bites confirmed it was every bit as tasty as it looked.

"Fresh coconut for dessert?" she asked hopefully.

"You bet," he returned. With a sailor's ease, he settled beside her. His foot casually caught hers, and giving it a friendly little waggle, he grinned and started in on his own meal.

Right now, Alix told herself, *is one of the happiest moments of my life. I intend to press this memory permanently into the scrapbook of my life.*

She leaned back, smiling at Ross.

He seemed to be intrigued by what he was seeing, for he studied her face long moments, until she began to feel self-conscious. Very seriously, he asked her, "What are you thinking?"

She shook her head. "We're all entitled to our secrets."

"Even if I press it, you're not going to tell me, are you?"

"Lunch's getting cold," she pointed out, and concentrated intently on her own.

"Okay, Alexandra. We'll drop it for now. But I intend to find out what that look meant."

From the sound of his voice, she knew that he suspected what her expression really meant, and he intended to confirm it.

If he thought for one minute that it was the look of a woman hopelessly in love . . . she had to admit to herself he was probably right.

Not that she'd slipped so far as to let it become blatantly obvious. She'd acknowledged the love she had been hiding even from herself. But she had been very sparing with her declarations ever since.

It was too new, too frightening. She did not feel comfortable or safe in abandoning herself to love. Slipping a delicately seasoned bite of the white fillet in her mouth, she said to herself wryly, *I'm not ready yet to try it without a net.*

What she was going to do was take it one day at a time. She was not going to think of the future —or of the past.

Ross reached out and gently brushed her arm. She set her free hand on top of his, acknowledging the gesture with a slight squeeze. It was amazing how tender this dynamic man could be. Alix found herself constantly wanting to forget the pressures of reality and simply bask in his loving attention.

And why shouldn't she? What harm could there be in taking this short time and savoring it? Each day Ross talked to her of trust, reassuring her of the permanence of his feelings for her. Even if that failed the test of time, why should she deny herself the pleasure of being with him now? She had just privately admitted this was one of the happiest moments of her life. She ought to be creating more of those moments to tuck away. Years from now she'd be able to take them out, unfold them, and warm her heart with sweet reveries of love.

In fact, she thought, looking out over the glassy surface of an increasingly calm ocean, why not create one such memory this very afternoon?

She flashed another smile at Ross. If her other grin had piqued his curiosity, this one ought to drive him positively crazy. She could see from the look in his eyes that he was intrigued, though he restrained himself from probing for an explanation.

She chuckled, a subtle little sound deep in her throat. Oh yes, love could be fun.

Alix sighed dramatically.

"It's *so* hot. Isn't it hot, Ross?"

Her back arched as she stretched with a long, languorous, deliberately sensual motion.

"Mmmm," he agreed, drinking in her catlike movement. "Maybe it would be wise to seek shelter." He glanced toward the companionway and the shadowed cabin below. "I'm sure we could find *something* to occupy ourselves down there."

"No." She frowned, now every inch the pouty

sex kitten. "It's too stuffy below. There's got to be a better way to cool off."

She began to amble in an apparently aimless fashion about the deck. As she moved, every step provocative, Ross seemed to forget he was supposed to suggest an alternative solution. His attention was riveted on her.

Standing by the wheel, she stared off over the brilliant blue water. She turned slowly, seeing the same curving blue horizon stretching around her forever. In the calm, the boat slid along at a steady diesel-driven three knots. They were alone in the world, a world that was nothing but an empty, flat disk, a sea-blue pancake beneath a domelike sky. As she completed her revolution, one hand reached out and flicked off the switch to the motor.

Silence invaded the ship as *Wind Shadow* slowed. Alix walked to the gunwale, picked up a line, and tossed the free end into the water.

Ross was watching her intently now. "Trouble?" he questioned.

She didn't answer. Instead she reached to her aqua cotton blouse and eased open the top button.

"Alix?" His question had a different tone to it this time. He stepped toward her.

One by one the buttons slipped open as she worked her way down the blouse. Ross stared transfixed as the last button surrendered.

Her fingers curved around the two open pieces

of cloth, spreading them slightly apart. Her legs moved. In two graceful movements she had kicked off her boat shoes. Then her hands slowly slipped the blouse off her shoulders and let it fall to the deck, leaving her naked to the waist.

Her fingers moved as though she were mesmerized, drifting to the fastening of her shorts. Her thumb caught on the brass snap of the white denim sailing shorts.

At the same moment, Ross's breath caught. She heard the small indrawn sound. With a sharp push, her thumb popped the snap open. It was followed by another slight choking sound from Ross.

He was only two feet away from her now. When the shorts followed the blouse, leaving her clad only in string-bikini-style panties of peach cotton, she finally looked him straight in the eye.

"What are you waiting for?" she asked, and, before he could react, dove over the side.

Down, down she plunged into a universe of transparent swirling blue. Then she was rising up through the silky waters to the light shining above.

Wind Shadow was drifting in the still air, barely moving. Her deck was empty.

Treading water, she turned to look around her. A yard behind was a foaming white circle of bubbles. Clearly Ross had accepted her invitation.

Realizing he was still below the surface, she guessed what would happen next, and drew in a deep breath in anticipation. Any second now she would feel his hand playfully gripping her ankle to yank her down into the water.

But her feet stayed free, lazily thrusting back and forth to keep her head above the surface.

An instant later, she discovered the nature of Ross's retaliation for her teasing.

It was the heat that first told her something was amiss. Instead of the slick coolness of the sea flowing over her breast, she sensed slick, heated, swirling contact there, a hot pressure that darted and probed.

Still sculling with one arm to keep herself afloat, she reached down. Her fingers caught in the swaying silver silk of his hair. Letting her hand slide down the back of his head, she caught his shoulder and eased Ross up to the surface. As he rose, his mouth and tongue continued to mark a searing trail over her skin, ending with a hundred ardent little nips along the sensitive cord of her neck.

Tiny shivers ran through her body, shivers that had nothing to do with the cool Caribbean currents.

Now his lips sought out hers. He covered her mouth, tantalizing her with his tongue as he outlined the line of her lips. Then he caught her lower lip between his teeth and nibbled at the ripe fullness.

Every so often his powerful legs would thrust, keeping them afloat in the buoyant salt water.

And all the while his hands, his mouth, drew her into that special timeless world of theirs.

When the heavenly kiss ended at last, Alix pushed away, swimming backward, her eyes fixed on Ross. She had the feeling that she was bewitched, transformed into a mermaid. She was a siren, luring her sailor to her side.

Sure enough, just as in the legends, he was swimming to her.

"No, Ross," she called out. "You can't come any closer."

She shook her head, and diamonds of water sprayed out. "Not unless you get rid of those shorts. This is a formal skinny-dipping party. No one admitted unless he's nude."

The diabolical grin of his that she knew so well spread wide. A few thrashing motions in the water and he was tossing his sodden shorts in a wild arc. They landed with a wet thud half on the rail, half on the deck.

Already his strong arms were slicing the water as he headed to her.

"Is that so, my mermaid?" he demanded as he reached her.

She discovered herself caught in an unbreakable grip. The feel of his arms around her filled her with delight. It bubbled along her veins, effervescent as champagne.

"Somebody"—his hand captured the curve of her hip—"here is cheating then." His fingers slipped beneath the elastic band of her panties. He pulled back, letting it snap.

She laughed. A deep, thoroughly happy sound.

He laughed too. Then his fingers twisted into the material and he whipped the wisp of cloth down her legs and off her. Raising the tiny wet peach triangle high above the water like a trophy, he swung it twice and let it fly.

It flew toward the boat, but fell short, landing with a small splash. As the scrap of material started to sink he made a motion to chase after it, but Alix held him back.

"Forget it."

She let her naked body slide against his, feeling the gentle current eddy around them. Her arms hooked around him. Her lips trailed along his neck, then worked their way up the jawline to his mouth.

"Ross?" she murmured.

"Yes?" His attention returned entirely to her.

"You know what?"

"No, what?" he answered her indulgently.

She reveled in the slide of his thighs against hers as he kicked to keep their heads above water. The blend of sleekness from the water and roughness from the hair on his thighs was deeply erotic to her. Now she knew what was right. She knew what she felt.

"I think—no," she corrected, "I know that I love you."

She was surprised how right it felt to speak the

words she'd held back on so many times over the past few days. As Ross responded with a hug that threatened to squeeze the breath right out of her, she laughed at the ease with which the words had slipped over her tongue.

"I love you. I love you. I love you," she cried, raining kisses on his water-slicked face, "love you, love you."

He leaned back from her enthusiastic display. "Truth?"

She knew he was concerned she was pushing herself, afraid she was glossing over the hang-up instilled by her father's desertion. She nodded solemnly. "I know what. I'm saying. I mean it from my heart. Truth."

He looked thrilled. Then he looked surprised. She imagined she did, too, since they had sunk beneath the smooth surface of the sea. They were staring at each other through a stream of white bubbles.

They kicked their way back to the surface. When Ross had finished choking out the seawater he'd swallowed, he declared, "Then there is only one thing left to do."

"What's that, my love?" Her own words were slightly roughened from the salty gulps she'd taken in.

"I will love you forever. I've told you that every day. Now I want you to let me prove it to you."

"Prove it? But, Ross, you don't need to prove it. I know it's true, I can see it in your eyes."

"You're going to see it right here." He caught hold of her left hand. "Let me put a ring there that pledges my love to you for eternity. Let me marry you, Alix."

If Ross had not been holding her, she knew she would have sunk down into the blue depths forever.

The idea was so frightening. Commitment, trust, promising forever. Could anyone really promise forever?

Alix was floating in a calm ocean, but within her was a maelstrom. Ross had pulled her close, and she sensed it was as much to grant her privacy, to shield her face—her thoughts—from him, as it was to show his love.

She had always run her life on the theory that she had herself alone to look out for or depend upon. She knew she loved Ross. She knew she wanted to be with him. But how could she learn to live with him? She and Ross were such independent, such determined, and self-directed people. Could two individuals so strong-minded learn to work together when it was required? It would be rough seas indeed if they couldn't.

She could feel his warm body against her, his arms holding her, as always, like the safest of harbors. The risks were there for them, no doubt about it. Marriage would not be easy. But more important, could she live without his love, now that she had experienced its wonders?

The answer, she knew, was no. She couldn't live without his love, and there was precious little point in pretending otherwise.

"Yes, Ross," she said to him, unaware of the tears coursing down her cheeks. "Yes. I will marry you."

CHAPTER TWELVE

Sunlight splashed over the verdant hills and over the town tumbling down the steep slopes into a cheerful jumbled heap at the water's edge. As if delighted by the sight, *Wind Shadow* romped toward the bright island.

"Hel-lo, Charlotte Amalie!" called out Alix.

It was the second time she'd sailed into St. Thomas's harbor this season, and the second time she'd greeted the place so enthusiastically. The first time she had been with Ross, and filled with the overwhelming joie de vivre that infects all couples who have just fallen in love. This time she was alone, but equally excited because she was sailing back to meet Ross after six interminably long weeks apart.

Though she and Ross had been forced to part ways temporarily to fulfill their chartering obligations, that miserable ordeal was over. Now, she grinned to herself as she whipped the wheel around, the duties were out of the way, and the decks were cleared for fun.

Long before she was close enough to the Sheraton Marina to identify any of the boats moored there, her eyes began straining for sight of *Sea Dreamer*. Ross would have his beloved boat back now. In fact, he would be preparing *Sea Dreamer* for their private rematch. Alix was pleased to be in love with a man who could appreciate a woman strong enough to compete with him. Love had not turned *these* two lions into meek little lambs. She and Ross had decided they would carry out their personal little challenge exactly as planned.

Of course there was also the Charter Boat League Annual Regatta to look forward to, she reminded herself. Thoughts of winning *it,* as well as their private race, had her humming as she sent *Wind Shadow* gliding through the crowded harbor.

Her good spirits were short-lived.

"What!" she was exclaiming to Ross an hour later as they sat in the hotel's coffee shop. *"Sea Dreamer* destroyed? You can't mean it."

"Jack's exact words to me when I called to check on the progress of the repairs three weeks ago were, 'She be up on the rocks, mon. She be high and dry.' "

"Ross, this is unbelievable."

"You're telling me?" His hand was running through his hair. "Damn storm blew up. She broke her mooring, and got washed up onto the rocks."

The news sent a hundred distressing thoughts

running through Alix's head. So many of his plans were ruined by this. What about his plans for occasional self-skippered charters on *Sea Dreamer?* What about the Charter Boat Regatta, and his shot at the prize money? What about insurance? Coverage for total destruction of a craft was very expensive. Many sailors chose not to carry that portion of a policy. Had Ross? If not, the loss of *Sea Dreamer* could mean financial disaster for him. What about the one-on-one race that was so important to them both?

And those were only the considerations. More important was how the loss was affecting her lover psychologically. Ross had a strong emotional attachment to his boat. Very common, as Alix knew from personal experience. Knowing how she felt about *Wind Shadow,* Alix could easily understand the sense of loss that Ross must be feeling.

Already she was gripping his hands, trying to convey her sympathy. But it didn't seem nearly comfort enough for her to offer. She wanted to give so much more—to wrap her arms around him, to hold him tightly and shelter him from the disappointment.

His voice was a slow, dull monotone. "It looks like all races are off, Alix."

"Yes," she answered, her eyes shining with empathy, "it does."

"Hey! What is this?" boomed a familiar voice. "I finally find the folks who've melted my

179

phone with their recitals of how they've started the biggest love affair since *Romeo and Juliet,* and what do I see? Act four of *King Lear.* What's the deal, guys?"

"Tully."

Alix turned to discover the bright, round face of her friend beaming at her.

"Tully," Ross echoed her, but his tone was dead, and he remained staring sightlessly ahead. Then he seemed to rouse himself.

"Sit down," he invited, holding out a hand to shake the man's chubby palm in greeting. "You might as well hear the great news too."

"I don't like the way you said that, Ross. Something's up. What is it?"

The chair scraped across the floor as Tully pulled the empty seat out and settled his short, pudgy form into it. He immediately propped one elbow on the table and rested his chin on his hand, head tilted, the epitome of a man prepared to hear every last detail.

"It's *Sea Dreamer.*"

"The rudder problem you told me about proving more hassle than you expected?"

"Worse. Another storm blew up after we left. She broke loose of her moorings and the wind blew her onto a coral reef. She's history—just one more casualty of the Caribbean."

"Oh, man." Tully loosed a long, sincere whistle of commiseration. "What are you going to do?"

"Not race tomorrow, that's for damn sure."

"*And* kiss your shot at a stake for your own charter firm good-bye," the rotund man added, referring to the prize money. He shook his head, his lips pursed in a moue of regret. "I'm sorry to hear that, buddy. Why, one of the reasons I flew out here was to see you two in action at this regatta."

Abruptly, Alix stood up. She couldn't stand it any longer. To watch Ross as he went through a postmortem of the destruction of his beloved ship, and the consequences, was more than she could bear. She shoved her chair back under the table.

"Would you both excuse me?"

To her discomfort, they both focused on her.

"I have some things to take care of," she said hastily. "Meet you back at your room, okay, Ross?"

Without waiting for confirmation, she landed a swift kiss on his lips and took off.

Ever a woman of action, she moved quickly. Unfortunately, she had no idea where she was going. Her head was too filled with unhappy thoughts to notice, and it wasn't long before she discovered she had brought herself back to the dock where she'd made landfall. There was *Wind Shadow* dancing lightly within the springer lines.

Maybe this was the best place to think, after all. Alix climbed aboard.

What was this disaster doing to Ross's ego? She couldn't tell, but then Ross was a man adept at hiding what he didn't want others to see. This charter regatta was very important to her, but she knew it was every bit as important to him.

For her, it was an opportunity to prove to the male-dominated sailing community that a woman was equally skilled at sailing. Winning against all those male skippers would prove it. It would give her prestige, would boost her reputation. That was the value to her, though the prize money would make the victory all the sweeter.

For Ross to win, she knew, would be an affirmation of the skills he was already acknowledged to have. It would entrench his reputation. Most important to him, it would provide funds for independent operation. He had been talking about the charter firm he wanted to start up. In their last days together he had spun great dreams of their future together, running that charter service.

Though Ross had lost *Sea Dreamer,* she still had *Wind Shadow*. She was set, registered in the race. She could invite Ross to crew for her—a humbling position she already knew was difficult for her independent man—and win the race. But it would be at the cost of his pride.

The only other option was to offer him *Wind Shadow,* to let him stand at the helm, with her as crew. Yet if she did that, she lost her platform for demonstrating the abilities of women mariners.

She had fought hard through the years to gain a reputation as a highly skilled captain among these male-oriented sailors. It had been the focus of her life. But was she willing to cement that reputation at the cost of her lover's spirit?

Alix stood before the hotel door, looking at the key that lay in her palm. The metal key felt cool, but her fingers were even cooler, icy in fact.

She had made her decision. Now all that was left was to carry it out.

Thrusting the key into the lock, she twisted it.

The door swung open. Ross stood by the dresser, turning his head in reaction to the sounds of the door unlocking. One instant they were staring at each other. The next, they were wrapped in each other's arms.

For a long, long time they held each other. Then Alix pulled her arms from around his back and let her hands slide onto Ross's biceps. She pressed, pushing herself away.

"We," she stated, looking into his face, "have to talk. I have an important proposition for you."

He let his arms drop away from her. "Maybe we'd better sit down for this."

Leading her to the king-size bed, he settled them both onto it. One bronzed arm stayed firmly tucked around her waist, the hand resting warmly on the curve of her hip.

She drew in a breath, praying that the sweetly scented tropical air would also contain an infusion of courage.

"I want you to sail *Wind Shadow* in the regatta."

She turned her head to look for his reaction. He seemed to be staring straight into her soul. "You want me to help you sail her?"

Her hand raised and arced in a gesture of denial. "No. I want you to skipper *Wind Shadow*. Take her, and win with her."

"What about your goal? What about proving that women are equal in sailing skills to men? I know from all we talked about during those last days of our voyage to St. Thomas that's very important to you. I know how much you want to prove it here at this race."

"There'll be other races. Do you think my ability to sail so well is transitory? I'll prove my point next year, never fear."

She was surprised then by his action. He dropped away from her, flopping back onto the bed. He lay, stretched over the brightly patterned spread, one arm crooked, with the forearm across his face.

The sight tore at her heart. She wanted to say something, do something. But she was frightened that whatever she did would make matters worse.

Had her offer insulted him? Humiliated him? Clearly he was upset. For five minutes she sat, caught up in knots, waiting in the silence broken only by the whisper of the breeze beyond the room and their own breathing.

On the sixth minute, driven crazy by the tension, she reached for him.

But Ross was already moving. His arm slid away from his face. He lay, staring at her.

"I had hoped that you loved me. But I never expected to be given proof like this. For you to sacrifice your opportunity for proving your worth, your chance to show all those chauvinist skeptics like me what fine, fine material you're made of . . ." He moved his head, a motion of denial. "And all to grant me—"

His voice stopped. A moment later it resumed, somewhat steadier.

"I let my own pride destroy my ship—ah *ah*," he cautioned, halting the objection she was just opening her mouth to voice.

"Don't say anything," he ordered. *"Sea Dreamer* would never have foundered on the coral reef if I hadn't damaged her in that storm first. The truth is, I don't deserve to sail in this regatta and you do. Yet here you are, willing to let me take your boat and scoop up the prize when I sail *Wind Shadow* to *your* victory."

His arms reached out to her, and she answered their summons. She lay across him, her head on his broad chest, her arms tucked along his sides, holding the man she loved.

"There is only one thing wrong here," he said as his fingers twined into the curls at the back of her neck.

"Uh uh," she replied, her lips barely brushing

against the soft knit of his cotton shirt. "Nothing wrong."

"Oh, yes there is. Your scenario gives me no chance to be noble. And if I can't be noble, then I won't be worthy of you. And, Alexandra my love," he assured her, his arms tightening until she almost couldn't breathe, "I'm not willing to accept a life without you. So you are going to have to be generous enough to let me turn your offer down."

"No." She struggled to sit up, but his arms gently held her in place.

"Yes. Now listen to me, Alexandra. I love you, and I owe you no less a sacrifice than you are willing to make for me. As wonderful as your offer is, it will bring us trouble later. What you're contemplating giving up is something so important to you that you cannot help but regret its loss. Eventually it will undermine our relationship. But most important, you are captain of *Wind Shadow*. You must be the one to sail her."

As she listened to Ross's words Alix felt a flood of love wash through her that brought tears to her eyes. How could she ever have doubted the depth of this man's devotion? His truly was a love to be counted upon.

"That's a hell of a speech, Captain Morgan," she murmured brokenly.

Again he hugged her. "I thought so," he teased in a love-soft voice. "Are you going to let me crew for you?"

"Do you really want to? I mean really? I know how independent you are."

"I think I'm tough enough to bear up under your command. You're not exactly Captain Bligh, you know." He tilted his head to capture her in a kiss.

She granted him the kiss, but then informed him, "I'm not exactly a cream puff, either. Don't go by our passage here to St. Thomas. That was cruising. This will be racing—and there ain't gonna be no slack cut for this baby."

"Yes, ma'am! That's the kind of talk I like to hear." With a swift motion, he rolled them over together, ending up firmly settled on top of her. "We're gonna win this one, sweetheart."

She looked up into his smiling face.

"Darling, I think we already have."

"Starboard tack, you day sailor, starboard tack!"

Annoyance sounded clearly in Alix's voice. She jerked the wheel, moving *Wind Shadow* so the craft sliding past her mere inches away did not graze the side of her boat. She could have let the ketch touch her boat. Since the skipper was clearly in the wrong, she would have been able to lodge a protest and have him disqualified from the race. But with little more than a minute to the start, it wasn't worth the risk.

As she zipped the wheel around once more to refill her sails and recover from her maneuver to avoid collision, she watched Ross expertly compensate for the boat's shifts. She drew in a breath and allowed her irritation to be washed away by the perfection of the sun, and the sea, and her ship, and its equally perfect crew. How could she fail to win this regatta with a mariner of that caliber as the other half of her two-sailor team?

"Great job, Ross," she called.

He raised his hand in salute. Then both of them were concentrating as Alix jockeyed for the best position for the start.

Hassel Island lay behind; the course lay ahead, a three-leg race. While setting up her "launch path" she recalled the beginning of her last race, when she and Ross had been swooping past one another. Racing was serious business. She'd been dead serious then; she was dead serious now. But what a delightful difference to be putting their talents together instead of pitting them against one another.

"What a skipper," Ross said, coming up beside her. He put an arm around her shoulder and gave a quick squeeze. "You've got us lined up perfectly."

She grinned at him. Then they were both focused on the sailing again.

Wind Shadow shot over the starter line a bare second after the gun went off. She was on a reach, and moving just as fast as the boats slicing the waves around her. They were to windward, an advantage for the free-masted ship.

By the time they were nearing the first mark, the minute island of Sand Key, only one boat was ahead of them.

"Lookin' good, sweetheart," Ross shouted from his position on the foredeck.

"You bet you are," she tossed back. This was one day she was definitely going to press the memory of in her scrapbook, she told herself. The kind of day a good sailor lived for, the kind of day a woman in love cherished.

The woman in love was still well satisfied when they bore down on the second mark, a coral reef. The sailor, however, was not quite so pleased. They had gradually been passed by other craft.

As she came around the reef she knew this was her last chance to gain the lead. It would be a straight shot downwind to Hassel Island. *Wind Shadow* was a past master at sailing wing and wing. The boat was bound to do well. But would it be enough to capture the lead?

"What do you think, Ross?" she asked a few minutes later. They stood together at the helm. In front of them *Wind Shadow*'s huge white sails splayed out on either side of the boat, flashing almost too brilliantly in the Caribbean sun.

"It's up to *Wind Shadow* now. But I think she can pull it off."

"Me too," Alix said with more confidence than she felt. There was little to do on this final leg of the race; she needed to distract herself. Yet she couldn't get her mind off winning, and the prize money that went along with it. And what that money would do for them.

She settled on one of the cockpit cushions, arm in arm with Ross. "Tell me about our charter firm again, the one we're going to start when we win this prize money."

"Well, to begin with, I've come up with a name since yesterday."

"You have?" She turned a curious face to him. "And what is it?"

"How do you like Wind Dreamer Cruises?"

Her smile was brighter than the sunlight glinting off the waves. "I love it, absolutely love it. A beautiful blend of our two favorite boats. Which reminds me, are you sure you want Jack to hold on to *Sea Dreamer* for you?"

Ross had told her the day before that he did have total coverage on *Sea Dreamer*. What a relief it had been to have that question answered positively, at least. It meant he could replace his investment.

"After all," she continued, "the insurance company has rated the boat totaled. They're buying you a new one. It'll take time and money to buy *Sea Dreamer* back from the insurance company and make the massive repairs she needs."

"I know. But I can't help feeling I owe it to her. Besides, when she's shipshape again, we'll have three boats in our fleet."

"Right. *Wind Shadow, Sea Dreamer,* and . . . ?"

"The *Love Boat?*"

Alix stared at him incredulously. "Men have been keel-hauled for less than that," she said. "If you dare to call your new boat *that,* even with tongue firmly in cheek, I'll . . . I'll . . ."

"What?" he laughed, capturing her in his powerful arms. "No, sweetheart," he assured her a moment later, after subduing her with a kiss, "whatever I come up with, it will reflect what we are together."

"Oh. Are you going to call her *Nitro,* or just *T.N.T.?*"

"How about *Love Forever?*" he asked, his voice so gentle she almost couldn't hear it over the sound of the waves. "Because that's what we share, you and I."

"Ross." She turned in his arms, embracing him. "I love you."

"Well, that's a very good thing, Alexandra Boudreaux. Because whether we win this race or not, you have definitely won a lifetime of loving from me."

And it was true.

Though they did win the race, and Mr. and Mrs. Ross Morgan soon established the Wind Dreamer Cruises yacht service with a fleet of three fine boats, in sharing their love, they had already won the best prize of all.